***"I've died,"** Luke said in a gravelly voice,*
"and gone to heaven."

His arms were holding her to him, their faces only inches apart. It didn't take much for him to close the gap. His hand, already cupped over the back of her head, exerted just a bit more pressure as he brought her mouth to his.

It wasn't the usual first kiss between strangers. There was nothing tentative or exploratory about it. He simply kissed Delilah with the casual familiarity and thoroughness of long habit, as if he were accustomed to finding her in his arms at daybreak. For one long, inebriated moment Delilah gave herself up to the kiss. Then, like a diver surfacing, she broke free, spitting fury.

"Just what do you think you're doing?"

His eyes full of laughter, Luke was now fully awake. "All right, not heaven, exactly. I never expected to end up there, anyway. But this'll do just as well." Before she could scramble off the bed and out of range, he caught her again, rolling her under him and giving her a quick, hard kiss, then releasing her, smiling recklessly.

Delilah jumped to her feet, gasping with anger and a breathless confusion she didn't quite understand. "If you do that again," she promised him fiercely, "I swear I'll pull out your stitches!"

WHAT ARE *LOVESWEPT* ROMANCES?

They are stories of true romance and touching emotion. We believe those two very important ingredients are constants in our highly sensual and very believable stories in the *LOVESWEPT* line. Our goal is to give you, the reader, stories of consistently high quality that may sometimes make you laugh, sometimes make you cry, but are always fresh and creative and contain many delightful surprises within their pages.

Most romance fans read an enormous number of books. Those they truly love, they keep. Others may be traded with friends and soon forgotten. We hope that each *LOVESWEPT* romance will be a treasure—a "keeper." We will always try to publish

LOVE STORIES YOU'LL NEVER FORGET
BY AUTHORS YOU'LL ALWAYS REMEMBER

The Editors

LOVESWEPT® • 139

Kathleen Creighton
Delilah's Weakness

BANTAM BOOKS
TORONTO • NEW YORK • LONDON • SYDNEY • AUCKLAND

DELILAH'S WEAKNESS

A Bantam Book / May 1986

*LOVESWEPT® and the wave device are registered
trademarks of Bantam Books, Inc. Registered in U.S. Patent
and Trademark Office and elsewhere.*

ISBN 0-553-21755-0

Published simultaneously in the United States and Canada

*Bantam Books are published by Bantam Books, Inc. Its
trademark, consisting of the words "Bantam Books" and
the portrayal of a rooster, is Registered in U.S. Patent
and Trademark Office and in other countries. Marca
Registrada. Bantam Books, Inc., 666 Fifth Avenue, New York,
New York 10103.*

PRINTED IN THE UNITED STATES OF AMERICA

O   0 9 8 7 6 5 4 3 2 1

For Winnie, my mother . . .
who knows all about sheep,
and the different ways to say "I love you."

One

"Mayday . . . Mayday, dammit, *Mayday!*" Luke Mac-Gregor snarled into his radio for the umpteenth time. He punched some buttons, then hung up in disgust. Picking up the telephone, he tucked it between his ear and shoulder, and put both hands on the controls of the single engine plane. He swore again, under his breath, as he felt the erratic vibration of the engine.

"Pete," he shouted into the phone, "are you still there?"

"Yeah. How are you doing?" The calm voice gave no indication of the tension Luke knew Pete, his foreman and longtime friend, must be feeling, far away in Mammoth with no power at all to help him out of this mess.

"Still flying," Luke said. "Just barely. Listen, I'm going to have to try to put her down. There's just no way I'm going to get enough altitude to make it over to Monache."

"What about Bishop?" the quiet voice on the other end of the line asked.

"I'm not even sure what direction Bishop is! My instruments are out. I could fly straight into the side of a mountain. Hey, listen. I've been circling a farm of some kind. Looks like a pretty good-sized pasture down there, from what I can see through these clouds. I'm going to try to get under them and take a closer look."

"Can't you at least find a road?"

"The roads all look like snakes from up here. And roads are apt to have fences. Barbed wire fences. Okay, I'm going down. . . . Uh-oh."

"What is it?"

"That pasture—it looks like it's full of *rocks!* Maybe I'll have to take my chances with the barbed wire after all. No, wait. The blasted rocks are *moving.*"

There was a patient silence on the line. The controls in Luke's hands were jerking violently now, and for a few minutes he was too busy to talk.

"Mac," Pete said tensely, "are you still there?"

Luke gave a dry, mirthless chuckle. "Yeah, I'm still here. Listen, I'm going to put this baby down in that pasture. Do a couple things for me, will you?"

"Sure thing, buddy." The hoarseness of suppressed emotion came across the airwaves and crackled against Luke's eardrum. He felt one electrifying shiver of fear and then went quite cold and calm.

"Tell Glenna I'm sorry I didn't make it to the wedding. I'll make it up to her somehow. Okay?"

"Gotcha. What else?"

A grim smile curved Luke's mouth as his hand closed around the receiver, ready to return it to its hook. "You might take a look at the insurance policy on this bucket. See if we're covered for sheep."

"*Sheep?*"

"So long, Pete. Wish me luck. I'll be in touch. . . ."

He hung up the phone and took the controls in both hands once again, wiggling his gloved fingers and shifting his shoulders as he drew one long, deep breath. "Okay," he said softly on its exhalation. "Move over, lamb chops. I'm comin' down!"

Delilah Beaumont was under the tarpaulin that protected her haystack from rain and snow, trying with wire cutters and clumsy gloved hands to find the wires that bound a bale of hay. In spite of the light dusting of snowflakes that was falling, she was hot, and sweat kept trickling down inside the collar of her nylon windbreaker, mixing with the leaves of alfalfa hay. She itched. Finally, swearing under her breath, she pulled the glove from her left hand with her teeth and probed for the wire with her bare fingers. In another few seconds she was backing out into the cold, fresh air of the March snowstorm with her arms full of hay, the glove still clamped between her teeth.

That was when she heard the plane. She had heard it circling earlier as she was going about her evening chores and had cast more than one puzzled glance at the lowering sky, wondering why an airplane would be circling her pitifully tiny place. She had no runway, unlike some of the larger ranches, with their rich absentee owners. And she'd been wondering, too, if airplanes were supposed to cough and sputter like that.

Now that intermittent cough was a deafening snarl, directly overhead. As Delilah stood with her arms full of hay and a ski glove hanging from her mouth, a bright orange airplane swept over her like a monstrous dragonfly, its wings waggling a little and then stabilizing, as if affirming its purpose. And its purpose, clearly, was to land in her pasture!

"*No!*" The sound emerged muffled, more as an inarticulate bellow. Delilah dumped both hay and glove into the waiting wheelbarrow and shouted again, "*No!*"

Then she was off and running as fast as she could, slipping on the wet, slightly uphill slope, ignoring the pasture gate and hurling herself over the fence so quickly, her feet barely touched the wires. She ran clumsily in her heavy waterproof boots, waving her arms frantically, the way one would try to shoo a hawk away from a brood of chickens. Her knit cap slipped down over her eyebrows, covering her short dark hair and most of her small, high-cheekboned face. She skidded to a halt, flushed and sweating, her breath coming in desperate sobs.

"No . . ." she cried, almost whimpered, as she stood

and helplessly watched the snarling orange monster from the sky reduce her precious flock of ninety-five pregnant ewes to a mindless, panic-stricken stampede. The entire flock broke for the dead end at the uphill side of the pasture and hurled itself against the heavy wire mesh fencing like lemmings against the last barrier to the sea. Finding that escape route blocked, the sheep scattered in ninety-five different directions, only to retreat again before the orange predator advancing upon them, landing gear outstretched like talons.

A small black-and-white bundle of spiky wet fur hurtled past Delilah's knees. She drew a deep breath and screamed, "Lady! Hold 'em, girl! Hold 'em!" and pointed toward the far end of the pasture. Immediately the border collie was streaking toward the flock in her herding crouch, ears flattened. The sheep apparently were more frightened and respectful of their ancient enemy and protector than they were of the new and unknown menace from the sky, because they stopped their witless dashing about and stood wild-eyed and stamping to face the dog's snapping, darting attack.

With her precious flock corraled, at least for the moment, Delilah turned her attention to the plane. In her concern for the animals it hadn't really occurred to her that the small, incongruously gay craft was in serious trouble. Now she simply stopped breathing, her bare hand clamped across her mouth, as she watched it touch the rough, tussocky ground and bounce, touch again on one wheel, slewing and skidding wildly across the pasture. With growing horror she saw the wheel hit something—a rock? a hole? a length of sprinkler pipe?—and crumple. The plane tipped, its wing brushing the ground, then slewed around and ground at last to a dead stop.

With a sound like that of a bucket of bolts being thrown into a fan, the engine protested . . . and then was silent. The propeller flapped around and around, and then it, too, was still. Her legs weak with apprehension, Delilah approached the plane.

As she came nearer, the cockpit door on the uphill

side of the tilted plane opened, and a pair of jean-clad legs appeared and flapped around, feeling for the ground. A moment later the rest of the body followed, hanging suspended from the cockpit door and then dropping with a muffled oath onto the soggy stubble.

Any relief Delilah had felt at seeing the pilot emerge under his own power faded in a rush of renewed dismay as he lurched to his feet and stood swaying beside the slanted wing. He was wearing a silver flight jacket—the kind with lots of zippers and a designer's name over the breast pocket—and it was rapidly becoming spattered with the blood that streamed down his face from a wound hidden somewhere in his thick chestnut-brown hair. Incredibly, he was smiling, a ruefully boyish Robert Redford grin that tugged at her heart in spite of the gory camouflage.

"Hi, kid," he said. He gestured toward the now-quiet flock, then used the same hand to grab at the airplane's wing for support. "Sorry about that. Had a bit of engine trouble. Your folks around?"

Delilah shook her head and stayed rooted where she was. Her mind was spinning frantically. She had already decided against panic, but the fact remained that the man was injured, and she wasn't equipped to render medical aid. She could handle almost any but the most complicated veterinary emergency and had a well-stocked medicine cabinet, but human beings were something else! What did one do for accident victims? All she could remember was something about keeping them warm. . . .

"Hey," the man said softly. "Look, son, I'm not going to drop dead, or anything. You don't have to look so . . . Oh, boy." He had touched his face and was looking at the dark stain on his glove. "No wonder you look so sick. Sorry." He probed experimentally at his scalp, and winced. "I guess I banged my head on something. This pasture is rougher than it looked from up there. Look, I'm going to need a little help. Go get your dad, okay, kid?"

Finding her voice at last, Delilah said gruffly, "I'm the

only one here, I'm afraid." Having him mistake her for a boy had had the effect of restoring both her wits and her anger. She decided not to enlighten him. Stepping forward, she put her arm around his slender waist and drew his arm across her shoulders. "I'm stronger than I look," she murmured when he protested. Keeping her own face averted from the mess of his, she leaned into his body, encouraging him to put more of his weight on her. She had to suppress a shudder. There was something disturbing about the dark eyes that glittered down at her.

Steady, Lilah, she told herself. It hasn't been *that* long since you were this close to an attractive man!

How did she know he was attractive? she wondered. She didn't know—unless it was that straight-toothed grin and the thick dark hair, glossy and clean where it wasn't wet with blood, and skillfully cut just long enough to suggest an air of devil-may-care. Or it may have been something else entirely—an aura of relaxed self-assurance that was downright awesome, considering the circumstances. It was the attitude of a man who was accustomed to being liked and admired, a man who was used to having his needs met, his orders obeyed—willingly.

Stiffening herself against automatic dislike, Delilah concentrated on the lean body she was half-supporting with her own. He was not a big man, thank goodness. Not terribly tall, not heavily muscled, just slender and naturally well built, broad of shoulder and narrow of hip and possessed of natural grace and coordination.

And how on earth did she know *that*? Was it just by the way his body moved against hers? The thought made her stumble, and she tightened her arm on his waist. He patted the shoulder he could reach and muttered thickly, "That's okay, kid, you're doin' fine. You really are stronger than you look, aren't you? How old are you?"

"Older than I look," Delilah said grimly. They had reached the pasture gate, and she had to release his waist and use both hands to untwist the double length of baling wire that kept the gate fastened. He shifted his weight, trying not to lean too heavily on her, and she heard the sound of his breathing, ragged in her ear. A shiver skittered over her neck and ran down her back.

"Not much farther," she muttered, taking up her burden once more. She noticed that his legs had developed a tendency to buckle. What would she do if he passed out here in the mud? How would she ever get him into the house? And what in heaven's name was she going to do with him once she got him there, anyway?

He did not, fortunately, pass out in the mud. Once inside her sparsely furnished but cheerfully cluttered little house, she helped him to a chair beside the kitchen table and left him to lower himself into it while she rummaged in a drawer for a towel. As she let the water run, waiting for it to become warm, she cast uneasy glances over her shoulder at the man, half-expecting him to topple out of the chair into a bloody heap at her feet. She watched him touch his scalp again, then he dropped his hand to the oilcloth covering the tabletop and looked about him with bright-eyed interest, taking in the richly colored Navaho rugs that warmed and softened the wood-plank walls and covered the threadbare patches on the secondhand sofa. When his wandering gaze encountered the rough Navaho loom beside the bookcase in the far corner, he turned to regard her with open curiosity and a touch of puzzlement.

"You all alone here, kid?" he asked as she approached him with the warm, wet towel. "Listen, I'm sorry about the sheep. I hope I didn't cause any damage."

"I hope so too," Delilah muttered. She caught her lower lip between her teeth and began to dab at the blood on his face. It was such a strange thing to be doing, washing a grown man's face, and a stranger's at that, that it had very little reality for her. She found that if she imagined him to be a small child, it was quite possible to steady his chin with one hand and draw the towel gently across his forehead, down the side of his face, and along the line of his jaw. But that jaw was pugnacious and stubbly, like no child's jaw she had ever seen. His eyes closed as the towel passed over them, and she saw that here, at least, in the long sweep of dark lashes, there was a kind of vulnerability that was *almost* childlike.

Her breath caught in dismay as fresh runnels of blood trickled across his forehead and onto the bridge of his nose. "You're still bleeding," she said, dabbing at the new stream. "I'd better take a look at that cut. Where is it?"

He pointed, tilting his head so she could reach the spot.

"Here," she said breathlessly. "Hold this." He took the towel and mopped at his face as she stepped closer, her fingers gently parting the blood-sticky hair as she peered at the injury. A three-cornered flap of scalp about the size of a postage stamp still welled darkly, just above his left temple. She shifted her gaze slightly and coughed as she encountered his bright eyes, just inches from her own. There was a frown between them, as if he were trying to remember something important.

She jerked involuntarily, and her fingers grazed the torn scalp. His breath hissed through his teeth, and he caught at her wrist, pulling her hand away.

"Sorry," she murmured. He was still holding her hand, staring at it, the frown deepening. Her gaze followed his. She saw a small, grubby hand, square and red-knuckled, with short, uneven nails. Not a pretty hand, true, but not the hand of a half-grown boy, either. She jerked it away.

"Uh . . . look," she said, tugging her knit cap farther down over her eyes, "that cut is going to need some attention. And I've got to get my sheep fed and shut up for the night. Do you think—" She hesitated, chewing at her lower lip and fighting with her conscience. Then, taking the towel from his hands, she folded it into a fat square and clamped it firmly over the injury, ignoring his inarticulate protest.

"Hold that—*tightly*," she instructed, guiding his hand to replace her own, noting, as she did so, the clean, square-cut nails, the long, graceful fingers, the slight roughness of calluses on the palms.

But, she told herself as she turned to the sink to retrieve her single glove, you can get calluses playing tennis and driving sports cars, too!

"Stay there!" she ordered tersely, turning at the door to give him a glare born of unreasonable anger. As she hurled herself out the door into the freshening snowstorm, she was fully aware that her anger was nothing but defense against guilt. She was leaving an injured man, to attend to a bunch of *sheep!* Surely, as these things are tallied in the celestial ledger, that must be a colossal blot in her debit column! But, darn it, those sheep were all she had. Her whole future was riding squarely on their fat woolly backs. And that man wasn't going to expire in her kitchen, not in the next half hour, anyway.

Up in the pasture she could see her flock still huddled against the far fence while Lady stood patiently on guard, her jaws stretched in a tongue-lolling canine grin. Delilah squinted at the darkening sky, gauging the time left before full twilight, and went to retrieve her glove from the wheelbarrow. Two more armloads of hay filled the barrow to top-heavy unwieldiness. She gathered her strength and pushed it doggedly uphill to the pasture gate. It was too muddy in the pasture for the heavy wheelbarrow, so she made several trips to deposit the hay in small piles across the lower end of the pasture.

"Okay, Lady, bring 'em down!" she called, and added the high-pitched and very distinctive cry she used to call the flock: "*Shoo . . . eee!*"

As the flock came hurtling down the slope in a single-minded rush for the hay, Delilah leaned on the gate and counted, watching for signs of ill effects from the stampede. As the sheep settled in small, busy huddles, she walked slowly among them, her fingers trailing lightly over an occasional damp, dirty gray back marked with streaks of colored crayon and the remains of last autumn's black numerals. Now and then a head was raised to stare at her—sleek black lop-eared Suffolk heads, with high-bridged, almost patrician noses, and the cold yellow sheepish stare, as flat and characterless as a stone. They all seemed fine. Some of them were so big they looked ready to give birth at any moment, but they were all fine—all ninety-five of them.

Delilah released a shaky breath, only now aware of just how worried she'd been, and went to feed the rams and milk the goats.

Half an hour later the ewes were once more shut securely in the holding pen, where open-sided shelters would provide escape from the worst of the wet spring snow.

Satisfied that for tonight the animals were secure, Delilah whistled for Lady and turned wearily toward the house. The heavy boots dragged at the muscles of her legs; the socks on her left foot had worked down and were bunched uncomfortably around her instep. Her nose was numb and her eyes were streaming from the cold; her fingers and toes ached with it. And worst of all, she itched.

And she still had to figure out what to do with the man who had fallen out of her sky.

Two

He was sitting where she had left him, the towel perched at a rakish angle over his left eye, his arms folded across his chest. The bleeding from his scalp wound seemed to have stopped. He watched her take off her cap and run her fingers through her short dark hair, then peel off the outer layers that made up her wintertime chore clothes: soaking-wet windbreaker, down-filled vest, waterproof boots. She was tucking the tail of her plaid flannel shirt into the waistband of her jeans, her movements pulling the shirt taut across the swell of her breasts, when she saw him purse his lips and nod his head. The blood-stained towel tumbled into his lap, and he caught it and tossed it onto the table.

"Thought so," he said without preamble. "Why didn't you set me straight?"

"About what?" Delilah avoided his eyes, for what reason she couldn't imagine. She had guessed he might be attractive; she was not prepared for *beautiful*. Cleaned up, his face was almost painfully handsome, though not the least bit pretty. It should have been a joy just to look at him, but when she did, she felt a surge of emotion she had decided must be anger. It certainly felt like anger. It quickened all her vital signs and made her fingers and toes tingle with adrenaline and her chest feel too tight.

In her experience, only rage had ever produced that particular constriction in her chest that made her want to shout at someone—anyone—just to relieve the tension.

"That you are neither a *kid* nor anybody's *son*," the man said softly.

Delilah shrugged, and dropped her soggy windbreaker across the back of a chair to dry. "At the time it didn't seem important. What difference does it make? You needed help and I was the only one here." She had moved to stand beside him, leaning over him to peer at his scalp. She felt rather than heard his chuckle as his shoulder bumped gently against her stomach.

"What *difference*?" he said. "*Vive*, as they say, *la différence!* Ouch." He had tried to turn his head to bring his eyes in direct line with her bosom. She tangled her fingers in his hair, restraining him none too gently.

"Hold still," she snapped, almost suffocating with that strange emotion. He had apparently washed his hair in the sink while she was outside. It was wet, but no longer sticky. "That cut needs attention," she said, frowning as she stepped away from him and picked up the stained towel. He had bled quite a lot. "You really ought to see a doctor." She gazed at him, chewing perplexedly at her lower lip, and he looked back at her, as relaxed and comfortable as if he had dropped in for coffee. He reached inside his jacket and took out a pack of cigarettes, and Delilah made a quick, involuntary motion of protest. She stifled it instantly, but he noticed it anyway.

"Sorry," he said as he tucked the cigarettes back into his jacket. "I won't if it bothers you. Are you allergic?"

Delilah shrugged ambiguously, guilt struggling with gratitude and the grudging beginnings of liking. She wasn't allergic; she just hated the smell of cigarettes. It clung to the wool in her rugs and blankets and was impossible to get rid of. But on the other hand, he was a guest in her house, and injured, and she was denying him his own comfort. And his sensitivity and courtesy were oddly unnerving. . . .

She gave a soft laugh and rubbed her palms nervously on her upper arms. "Look, I'm sorry, but I don't know what to do with you. I'm not . . . very experienced at dealing with the victims of plane crashes—"

"Please. That was a perfectly executed emergency landing!"

"—in my pasture! Emergency landing? Well, couldn't you have found a . . . a less *populated* place? You could have wiped out my flock! Everything I own!" She hadn't known she was going to cry. Her voice had simply escalated with each sentence, until she was very close to that tension-relieving shout she had longed for. The tears just seemed to go along with it.

The man's dark eyes crinkled sympathetically. "I'm sorry. From up there it looked like the best place. Are they okay?"

"Yes." She sniffed grudgingly, touching her nose with the back of her hand and then reaching absently for a tissue. "I think so. I'll have to check more closely. They're only a week or so away from lambing," she explained in muffled tones, beginning to feel thoroughly ashamed of herself.

His straight, dark brows dipped, and he made a low whistle. "I don't blame you for being upset. Do you really live here all alone? Run this place by yourself?"

"I *own* it," Delilah said stiffly.

Again that low whistle. The brown eyes seemed to be laughing at her, though the beautifully shaped mouth was carefully somber. "Big job for a little bit of a girl."

Genuine anger coursed through her, wiping out the other, more confusing emotions. "In the first place, I'm not a girl, I'm a woman. And if I hear one more arrogant, insufferable man tell me a woman can't make a go of it in the sheep business, I'll . . . I'll—"

"Hey, take it easy." He was laughing at her, sympathetically and without a trace of arrogance. "I didn't know I was probing an open wound. Speaking of which—"

"How did you figure it out?" she interrupted suddenly as a much-delayed thought occurred to her.

"What?"

"That I wasn't 'anyone's son'?"

He smiled, the same heart-squeezing smile he had bestowed on her through riverlets of blood. On a clean face it had an almost angelic beauty. She suddenly found it a chore to remember to breathe.

"Instincts," he said, his voice acquiring a new resonance that raised goose bumps on her arms. Then he chuckled, releasing her from the magnetic pull of his personality as if he'd turned off a switch. "Of course, once I went exploring and saw—"

"You went exploring?" Her voice was a squeak. "In my house?"

"Don't get excited. I'm not planning to rip you off. I was looking for a bathroom, a telephone, and an ashtray, in that order. I found the bathroom. I think." He shook his head in disbelief. "I've never seen more primitive amenities indoors. Do you really shower in there, on that cold cement floor? Without heat?"

"Sorry," Delilah said faintly, thinking of what was hanging on the curtain rod in the bathroom. "If you don't like the accommodations you can always try the motel down the road."

"I apologize . . ." he murmured, but it was Delilah who felt remorse. His long lashes swept down for just an instant, and she noticed that he'd taken on a grayish pallor, and the delicate skin under his eyes looked bruised. He was injured and had been through a harrowing experience, and all she had done so far was fence with him, she thought guiltily. What was the matter with her?

She spread her hands. "I don't have a telephone," she said.

"No phone." He took a deep breath. "I hate to ask, but is there any chance you could give me a lift to the nearest town? Preferably someplace with a hospital? And a telephone. I don't want—"

He stood up abruptly. Delilah wasn't watching him at that moment—her eyes were focused on nothing as she chewed her lip and contemplated the prospect of putting chains on her Navy surplus pickup in the cold, muddy darkness. So she was completely unprepared when he did, at last, pass out at her feet.

He went down like a bag of bricks, not in graceful slow motion, as people do in the movies. He hit the floor with a sickening thud and then sort of flopped, full length and face down.

"Oh . . . *no*," Delilah breathed, and dropped to her knees beside the inert body. Overcoming a strange reluctance to touch him, she put her hand on his shoulder and gave it a gentle shake. She almost changed her mind about allowing herself to panic. Fear clutched at her throat like a cold hand, but she wrestled gamely with it and fought it off. He'd just jumped up too quickly, that was all, she told herself. He'd lost quite a bit of blood, and it was warm in the room, and he had stood up too fast. He was weak and needed rest. He was going to be all right.

She shifted her position, braced herself, and rolled him over, surprised at how heavy he was now that he was dead weight. Moving him wasn't going to be easy. Sitting back on her heels she contemplated the face of the man who was making such a hash of her already precarious existence. Even slack in unconsciousness the features were remarkably fine. It was in the bones, she decided. He would be a handsome man even when he was old. Right now, though, there was a dark stubble on the lower half of his face, a shiny film of sweat on the upper half, and purple smudges just below the fringe of dark lashes. Odd, she thought. He seemed both more and less disturbing like this. Without the force of personality behind him he wasn't nearly so potent an assault on her senses, but with her guard lowered he seemed to be launching some sort of clandestine flank attack on her heart. . . .

With a gentleness that would have amazed most of the people who knew her, Delilah smoothed the hair back from his forehead. Her fingers went automatically to the laceration in his scalp, and came away stained with blood. The fall must have started it bleeding again. When she got to her feet and opened the cupboard that held her store of veterinary supplies she knew she had made a decision. This man, whoever he was, was in no condition to go anywhere tonight.

A few minutes later she had settled herself on the floor with his head in her lap, a small assortment of objects arranged at her elbow. As she poured hydrogen peroxide into the wound and watched it foam and fizz, she considered alternatives for dressing it. It was in an awkward place. The only possibilities seemed to be to shave a big enough patch on his scalp to stick Band-Aids to, or to sew the torn edges together. She knew she would never be able to bring herself to cut a hole in that thick chestnut hair. Resigned, she fished out of a little dish of alcohol a needle already threaded with dental floss, took a deep breath, and began.

It took seven stitches to close the wound. He woke up in the middle of the third one. Delilah saw his eyelids flutter and felt tension return to his neck and shoulder muscles, but she clamped her lower lip firmly between her teeth and finished the stitch. The brown eyes flew open.

"I'm on the floor," he said thickly.

"Right," Delilah confirmed absently. "Hold still, please."

He wrinkled his forehead, trying to see her face. "What're you doing?"

"Sewing you up. Please don't make me nervous. I've never done a human being before."

"Never . . . done . . . a human *being*?"

"Just sheep and dogs. But I'm pretty good, and I have antibiotics, if you're worried. Are you up on your tetanus shots?"

"Uh . . . yeah. Listen—"

"*Hush.*" Delilah clipped off the next stitch. "You passed out. You are in no condition for a thirty-mile run to town in a snowstorm. You can stay here tonight. Tomorrow I'll get you to a phone, I promise. I'm as anxious as you are to get that plane out of my pasture. But right now, *please* be still, before I lose my nerve completely. Better yet—go back to sleep!"

A slight smile flickered over his lips, and he closed his eyes. "Right, doc." He sounded groggy. Delilah sucked in her breath and completed another stitch. He didn't flinch. She finished the job and dropped the needle back into the dish.

"All done," she said huskily. She couldn't resist passing her hand across his forehead once more, her fingers combing back an errant lock of hair.

His eyes opened and found hers. "Feels good," he murmured.

"Having your *head* sewn up?"

Again that faint smile. "Having your satin fingers soothe my fevered brow, Florence Nightingale. You have a nice touch."

His voice was soft and musical, with a slight rasp to it that stirred odd harmonics deep inside her. She cleared her throat and took his head in her hands to lift it from her lap. His hand came up to catch at her wrist.

"I've . . . I've got to get up," she stammered. "Fix you a bed—"

"I'd just as soon stay right here," he muttered, holding her hand against the side of his head. She felt her fingers curl involuntarily into the crisp silk of his hair.

Oh . . . 'Lilah—what's the matter with you? she asked herself. You don't even know this guy's name. Get up, you idiot!

"Let me up," she said, more harshly than she'd intended, and slid out from under him, out of his grasp, away from the insidious warmth that was invading her body.

He sighed and slowly raised himself to a sitting position, feeling gingerly for his injury.

"Leave it alone," she snapped. "You'll infect it."

He gave a soft chuckle and leaned back against the table leg. Delilah felt his gaze follow her into the cold bedroom, but when she went back to the kitchen his eyes were closed. She wondered if he had dozed off, wondered if she should be trying to keep him from sleeping. But no—wasn't that for concussion? His injury wasn't from a blow, it was a cut, with considerable loss of blood. Sleep was what he needed.

"Come on," she said. "I've a bed ready for you."

He held onto the table leg and managed to regain his feet, but he seemed dazed and unsteady as he followed her into the bedroom. He sat heavily on the edge of her double brass bed, and she saw again the ominous gray under his tan, the faint sheen of moisture on his forehead.

"Are you going to be sick?" she asked suddenly.

"No . . ." he said, and keeled over sideways onto the pillows. Delilah made a small whimpering sound of exasperation and pondered the fully dressed form of the man—a total stranger, for Pete's sake! Then she sighed and reached for a booted foot. There was just no way she was going to put all that mud and blood onto her clean sheets!

She undressed him, clinging to her exasperation like an amulet and not lingering over the task. She left him in a soft blue pullover and undershorts, and jerked the flannel sheet and quilts up to his chin. Only then did she realize that her hands were shaking. Delayed reaction, she thought, draping his jeans over the rocking chair and arranging the boots under it. She gathered the blood-stained jacket and damp socks into a bundle and left him.

Surprisingly, the care label on the jacket proclaimed its washability, so she put it in a sinkful of cold water to soak. How odd it seemed to be moving around the big, warm, familiar room that was a combination of living room, dining room, and kitchen, putting on a Simon and Garfunkel record, taking a jar of peanut butter, an apple, and a pitcher of goat's milk out of the refrigerator, and sitting down at the table, and opening her ledger books, just as she did every night. For heaven's sake, there was a strange man asleep in her bed, a crippled airplane in her pasture!

Delilah gave an astonished laugh and scooped a large spoonful of peanut butter out of the jar. As she nibbled absently at it, she ran her finger down the untidy column of numbers in the ledger, counting under her breath. The figures and notations were in several different types of ink as well as pencil and crayon, and were marred by frequent crossing-outs and margin jottings. They would have meant absolutely nothing to anyone else, but to Delilah they were confirmation of what she already knew—that in a little more than a week, give or take a couple of days, the first of ninety-five ewes would lamb. The latest lambs would have arrived at the end of a month's time. The interim three weeks would be a nightmare of backbreaking work and sleepless nights. Could she do it alone? Last year she had sometimes wondered whether she'd make it, and she'd had only fifty ewes.

Pushing the ledger away, Delilah laced her fingers behind her head and stared at the wood-plank ceiling. She *had* to manage; that was all there was to it. This was the critical year. If she didn't break even this year, she was finished. Her father would say, "I told you so," and Amos could have her land and her precious water rights. She would finally get the comeuppance a lot of people had been predicting for years.

There was some stomping on the front doorstep, followed by a rapping on the door. Delilah cast a quick glance out the window, where an official black-and-white car with a light bar on the roof waited, lights on and windshield wipers thumping, and called out, "Come on in, Roy."

A tall blond man in sheriff's-department khakis, cowboy hat, and a fur-collared leather jacket stuck his head in the door.

"Evenin', Delilah. I'm pretty muddy."

Delilah waved impatiently from her seat at the table. "Come on in here, Roy. You know I don't get excited about a little mud. Come have a cup of coffee. Still snowing?" She got up to reach for the kettle, but the deputy waved her back as he came in and shut the door behind him. He took off his hat but stayed where he was, with one hand on the doorknob.

"Can't stay. Yeah, it's coming down pretty good—not

sticking, though. Just wet and soggy enough to make a mess of the roads. Say, listen, I'm trying to run down a missing plane. Had a report from Mammoth. Thermodyne says one of their bigshots is down, and was last heard from in this general area. I was just over at Amos's, and he says he thought he heard a plane go over about chore time, flying low. Thought maybe you might have heard something."

Delilah smiled smugly and pointed with her peanut-butter-coated spoon. "I can do better than that. The plane's up in my pasture."

Deputy Sheriff Roy Underwood's head jerked in surprise, and then he grinned. "*Shoot.* I mighta known. Pilot?"

Again Delilah used her spoon as a pointer. "In there."

"Well, I'll be damned. Hurt?"

"Not much. Just a scalp wound. I sewed him up, but he'd lost quite a bit of blood and was pretty shaky. I didn't want to try to drive him out in this storm."

"Dammit, Delilah, when are you going to get a phone?" The deputy was moving toward the bedroom door, his lawman's paraphernalia clanking softly. He paused with his hand on the doorknob to give her a wondering look. "Sewed him up, huh?" He chuckled and stuck his head into the bedroom, looked for a long moment, then withdrew, pulling the door carefully shut.

"I'll be damned," he muttered. "Guess I can take you up on that offer of coffee after all." He tossed his hat onto the table. "You know, some worried people are going to be awfully glad to hear about this. In fact—" He snatched his hat back and turned to the door. "I'll go get this on the radio and then shut down. I'm about due for a break."

He disappeared into the snowflakes, and Delilah put a kettle of water on to boil. By the time Roy had returned, stamping his feet and shaking snow off his hat, the water was hot and the jar of instant coffee was sitting on the table beside two cups and the sugar bowl. She and Roy both liked their coffee black and sweet.

"Ah, looks good. Thanks." Rubbing his hands

together, Roy hitched a chair back and sat down. "Sure is nice to have something like this turn out all right for a change."

"Who is he?" Delilah asked, trying to sound casual. "You mentioned Thermo . . . something."

"Thermodyne—the company that's doing the geothermal drilling up near Mammoth Lakes. From what I gather, this guy's the company's founder, chief engineer, and president. Name's . . ." He took a piece of paper from his shirt pocket, peered at it, and tucked it back. "MacGregor. Luke MacGregor." He grinned suddenly, jerking a thumb toward the bedroom. "Goodlooking guy. I have to say, he looks right at home in your bed, Di."

Delilah made a face. "You're as bad as Mara Jane. And don't you start on me, either," she added warningly as he opened his mouth to comment. "I've heard all I want to hear about how this place is too big and the job's too tough for me, and I need a *man*!"

"Whether or not the job's too big for you's got nothing to do with it. *And*," Roy said emphatically, pointing a finger at her to silence her retort, "don't give me that male-chauvinistic, Cinderella complex bull, either! That's not what I mean, and you know it. People just weren't meant to go it alone. A woman needs a man, just like a man needs a woman. That's a fact of nature."

"Bull . . . feathers," Delilah said succinctly.

"Bull *nothin'*. Delilah, just look at Mara Jane and me. Now, you sure can't say I've held her back or kept her from doing what she wants to do, can you? Hell, with Mara Jane always off to New York or L.A. for talk shows and writers' conferences, I bet I've changed more diapers than she has. And I make better pancakes. Mara Jane's had all the room she needs to be who she wants to be, and she still shares a pretty damn good life with me!"

"You two are just the exception that proves the rule. Let's face it, Roy, any man with an idea of hooking up with me is either going to want to move me off of this place or take it over. And there's no way I'm ever going to let anybody do either one. This is *my* place, *my* land.

Roy, I've wanted to be a rancher all my life. Not the wife of a rancher—a *rancher*. I'm one-eighth Navaho, did you know that? Maybe that's got something to do with it, I don't know. I bought this land with Indian money—my mother's, my grandmother's, and my own share combined. I threw my whole stake into this land and the nucleus of my flock, and I figured I had enough money to support me through three building years. This is the third year. I figured with a hundred ewes I could break even, if the market holds steady and I'm very frugal and have a good crop of lambs. Well, I've got ninety-five ewes, thanks to that coyote trouble I had last year. So I'm on thin ice anyway, and I get very defensive when anyone tells me I shouldn't be doing this!"

"Yeah, I know." Roy drained his mug and stood up. "Lambing time coming up, too, right? Getting any help this year?"

Delilah smiled tiredly. "Now, you know I can't afford a hired man."

"Amos Chappel tells me he offered you one of his men and you turned him down."

"And that surprises you? Good old Amos!" Delilah gave a short spurt of laughter. "You and I both know what Amos Chappel wants. And you wonder why I get touchy on the subject of men. He wants this place for the water in that creek, Roy, and you know it."

"Sounds like a John Wayne movie," Roy said, laughing. "Why is it so hard to think he could be interested in *you*?"

"You sound like one of Mara Jane's books. Amos never cared for anything but a dollar in his life."

"Then, wouldn't he be better off to let you struggle? Fall flat on your—"

"He's sure that'll happen sooner or later anyway, and he's just dumb enough to figure I'll be so beholden to him I'll fall right into his arms."

"Delilah," Roy said, clamping his hat onto his head, "how did someone so young, and so pretty, get to be so cynical?"

"Try being young, pretty, and *female* sometime, Roy,"

she retorted. "That and a dime will buy you a lot of grief, and not even a way to telephone for help. All people do is use that as a reason to keep me from doing the things I want to do. Go home, Roy. I'm tired and I want to go to bed—*on the couch*," she added pointedly at his guffaw, and threatened to throw her cup at him.

Three

Luke MacGregor, founder and president of Thermodyne, Inc., was still asleep in Delilah's bed when she
went out to do her chores at the crack of a cold, slushy
dawn. In fact, it looked to Delilah as if he had barely
moved since she had tucked the quilts under his chin
the night before. After graining the ewes in the holding
pen, lugging three heaping loads of hay in the wheelbarrow to the pasture, carrying hay and water to the rams'
pen, and feeding, watering, and milking the two goats,
Delilah went back to the house for breakfast and
decided to look in on her patient again. She was beginning to worry about him. She didn't know what consti-
tuted normal postplane-crash behavior, but she had
never seen anyone literally sleep like a *rock*.

Well, he had moved, at least, she thought when she
entered the bedroom. He had rolled onto his side,
toward the wall, where an anemic March sunrise was
crystallizing the moisture-fogged window. Delilah
approached the bed timidly.

"Mr. MacGregor?"

There was no answer. She gazed perplexedly at the
quilted mound, the feathers of chestnut hair, and
gnawed at her lower lip. Was he all right? He wasn't even
snoring. It made her very nervous to have him continue

to sleep like that. For the first time she began to question the wisdom of her decision to keep him here rather than drive him to a hospital. She hated to disturb him, but she needed reassurance. Bending over, she cautiously touched his shoulder and repeated softly, "Mr. MacGregor . . . wake up."

There was a prolonged exhalation—not quite a yawn, not quite a groan—and an arm emerged from the blankets to hook carelessly over her neck.

Caught off-balance and completely by surprise, Delilah gave a small squawk and collapsed onto the bed. Luke rolled toward her as his other arm came out of the covers, and he wrapped both arms securely around her. With a contented and completely unintelligible murmur he cuddled her close to his body, one hand cradling her head and tucking it firmly into the warm curve of his neck.

Delilah held herself very still, half-suffocated with incipient panic. She told herself that there was no reason to panic, that it was, in fact, an extremely humorous situation. Someday, probably, she would tell the story and chuckle heartily. At the moment, though, she was in no position to appreciate fully the comic aspects of her predicament. She was much too busy trying to remain calm enough to figure a way out of it.

Calm, reasoning analysis of the situation—that was what she needed. Obviously, he was asleep and didn't know what he was doing. Probably he had mistaken her for someone else. She rather doubted that a man who looked as he did was accustomed to waking up alone. He could even be married. All right. So far, so good. But the question was, could she get loose without waking him up? She moved experimentally against the restraining bands of his arms. *No.* The answer to that was definitely no. His arms tightened, holding her even closer.

She relaxed, momentarily accepting defeat, and a very strange thing happened. She realized that her position wasn't at all uncomfortable. It was, in fact, extraordinarily enjoyable. There was something insidiously seductive about being surrounded by the vibrant warmth of a male body, the unfamiliar yet wholly pleasant scent of an essentially clean, well-groomed healthy man just waking up in the morning—a musky scent more intoxicating than the most exotic cologne.

His stubbly chin rasped across her forehead. "Mmmm," a low, husky voice murmured. "Your face is cold. Whatcha been doing?"

Delilah clamped her teeth on her lower lip. She put her hand flat on his chest and managed to lever her head up. "Mr. MacGregor—"

Chestnut eyes fringed with black stared intently into hers. "I've died," Luke said in that gravelly voice, "and gone to heaven."

She was already only inches away; it didn't take much for him to close the gap. His hand, already cupped warmly over the back of her head, exerted just a bit more pressure and he brought her mouth to his.

It wasn't the usual first kiss between strangers. There was nothing tentative or exploratory about it. He simply kissed her with the casual familiarity and thoroughness of long habit, as if he were accustomed to finding her in his arms at daybreak. And maybe because of that quality of familiarity, or maybe because she was just too shocked to resist, for one long, inebriated moment Delilah gave herself up to that kiss. And then, like a diver surfacing, she broke free, spitting fury.

"What the . . . *hell* do you think you're doing!"

His eyes laughed at her, wide awake now. "Oh, well. *Not* heaven, then. That's okay. I never really expected to get there anyway. This'll do just as well." Before she could scramble off the bed and out of range, he caught her again, rolling her under him, his hands pinning her shoulders to the pillows as his quilt-cocooned body trapped and held her helpless. He gave her a quick, hard kiss, then released her, laughing as she rolled away and lurched drunkenly to her feet.

"If . . . you ever do that again . . ." she said with a gasp, boiling mad and fighting tears of confusion and rage, "I swear I'll . . . I'll *pull out your stitches!*"

She stalked from the room, trying to pretend that

nothing out of the ordinary had happened to her. As she slammed cupboard doors, banged pots, measured rolled oats and water—remembering in the nick of time to double the usual amounts—she kept telling herself, as if reciting a mantra, He was asleep. He didn't know what he was doing. It meant absolutely nothing.

But she was left with the lingering essence of both the man and the kiss, more vivid in a way than the real thing. At the time she had been too surprised, too embarrassed, too angry, to be aware of the assault on her senses. *Now* she felt the tingle of her skin where his beard had rasped against it, the moisture on her lips from his mouth, no matter how hard she tried to rub it away. And no amount of rubbing could dispose of the tactile memory of his hand on the curve of her skull, his lips, firm and warm, fitting themselves so perfectly over hers, his tongue sliding over her teeth, surprising her so that she opened her mouth to him. . . .

Her stomach churned audibly, and she pressed her hand against it. Hunger, that was all it was, she told herself, furiously stirring the bubbling oatmeal, not even thinking about the fact that there was more than one kind of hunger.

There was a sound—or maybe just a subtle alteration in the room's vibrations sensed on another level entirely. Delilah turned to find her houseguest standing in the bedroom doorway, tucking in the shirttail of his blue pullover and watching her quizzically.

"I wish I could say I'm sorry about that." His husky voice touched the back of her neck as she hastily returned to the steaming pot. "But I'm not. That's just about the best way I can think of to start a new day." His voice gave away his smile. "In fact, I think I'd like to try to arrange it as often as possible."

"Like room service?" Delilah said brightly, removing the pot from the stove and clapping a lid on it with unnecessary force.

"Why not?" He *was* smiling—not that sweet, beautiful smile that had the power to knock her silly, but a crooked grin holding more than a touch of puckish mischief. "What's the matter—never tried it . . . or don't like it?"

"Both," she said firmly, "with strangers."

"Ah, but I'm not a stranger." His eyes twinkled at her through a fringe of black. Delilah had an idea those eyes were probably registered somewhere as lethal weapons. "You saved my life. Well, sewed up my head, anyway." His voice softened. "I just spent the night in your bed. And"—he paused to look around the room and back to her—"*someone* undressed me." He came toward her, and she eyed him the way a rabbit watches a fox. "*And* you know my name. I heard you."

"You *heard* me! You . . . I thought you were asleep!"

His only answer was a soft ripple of laughter. Glowering furiously, deliberately avoiding both him and his gaze, Delilah fetched and bustled and slammed, moving back and forth from counter and stove to table, setting out bowls, cups, spoons, milk, sugar, instant coffee, and last, on a hot plate to protect the oilcloth, the pot of oatmeal.

"Breakfast," she announced, wondering why she felt so surly and ungracious this morning. "If you want it."

He lifted the lid of the pot and sniffed as if intrigued. "Oatmeal. Haven't had that since I was a kid. Used to eat it with raisins," he added hopefully.

"Raisins," she said shortly, "are expensive." He was standing close to her, blocking her way to the table. Her breath was short and her stomach was growling. She was hungry again, she thought. "Please," she said, almost desperately, "sit down."

"You don't like to kiss a stranger; I don't like to eat with one," he said softly. "Tell me who you are."

"What?" She stared at him, unaccountably confused. That simple question, in that curiously husky murmur, seemed to carry a much, much more complex command. A command to strip herself naked for him, figuratively speaking; to bare her very soul. *Tell me who you are.* . . . Instinctively she drew her natural reserve around her like a cloak.

He laughed. "Your *name*. Tell me your name. It's only fair—you know mine."

"Um . . . sure. It's Delilah. Delilah Beaumont."

"Delilah . . ." He rolled the name around on his tongue, and then seemed to do a double take on her last name. "*Beaumont?*" he asked sharply, and when she nodded he muttered something under his breath and shook his head wryly. "How did you know my name, by the way?" he asked, cocking his head sideways. "Run through my pockets while I was out cold?"

She studied him with distaste. "Your wallet and the other contents of your jacket are over there." She pointed to the counter. "I washed the blood out of your jacket. I didn't think you'd want it ruined. It looked expensive. For your information," she went on quietly, rather enjoying the mild chagrin that flickered across his face, "the sheriff came by last night, looking for you. He has notified your next of kin, Mr. MacGregor."

Luke puffed out his cheeks and blew a gust of self-reproach, shaking his head and hooking his hand on the back of his neck. "Sorry," he murmured. "That was uncalled-for. Thank you. Belatedly, wholeheartedly . . . thank you. For everything. For having your pasture in just the right place, for your strong shoulder, your silken fingers, your needle and thread, your bed, and for getting the word out on my probable survival. And thank you . . . for having the most incredible pair of eyes a man ever woke up to."

There it was again, that angel's smile, that voice with those crazy suspensions that tingled through her auditory canals and right on down her spine. He could turn them both on and mesmerize her without even trying. Or *was* he trying? Was he so used to charming people that he considered he owned right of conquest to everyone he met? The man was dangerous, she decided. He shouldn't be allowed out in public unless properly shielded!

See? she went on silently. Somehow there he was, standing too close to her, one hand on the back of her neck, and she couldn't for the life of her think how he had gotten there. She licked her lips. His fingertips were skimming lightly over the fine dusting of hair on the back of her neck.

"Your hair, your skin, your cheekbones . . ." he murmured. "You ought to have midnight eyes. Instead they're like a winter morning—ice blue, with a nice warm fire inside. Have you always worn your hair short like this?" His fingers brushed at the feathers of hair on her forehead, touched her cheekbones, and then slid down to join his other hand at the back of her neck.

"No," Delilah said hoarsely. "It's a form of rebellion. Men prefer long hair."

"But *I* don't. This suits you perfectly. And it frames your eyes. . . ."

"I'll grow it out first thing tomorrow," she said, her voice choked. She dove under his arm and surfaced outside the perimeter of his spell. "Look," she said, speaking lightly, rapidly, "I always thought it was supposed to be the Irish who were masters of blarney, not the Scots! I've got a lot of work to do, and I've been up for hours already. I'm hungry. I'm going to eat my breakfast. After which I still have a few things to do before I can take you down the mountain. So if you mean to get back to civilization today, you'd better get out of my way and let me eat my breakfast."

She pulled back a chair and dropped shakily into it, surprised to discover that her legs were weak. As she helped herself to a dollop of now-congealed oatmeal, poured milk over it, and poked doggedly at it, she heard a soft ripple of laughter and the bathroom door clicking shut. She dropped the spoon and collapsed back in her chair, expelling a long-held breath. She felt as if she had just pushed a loaded wheelbarrow the entire length of the pasture. Uphill.

"Brr," Luke said awhile later, rubbing his hands together as he emerged from the bathroom. "Do you keep it that cold in there for a reason?"

"Several, actually," Delilah said, deadpan, her sense of humor returning with her self-control. "Discourages loitering, and puts roses in your cheeks." Ignoring his surprised and appreciative hoot, she went on. "You see, this house started out as a line shack. No plumbing or electricity. Someone added that bathroom by simply partitioning off a part of a storage lean-to and pouring a concrete floor. Period. There's no insulation in there at all."

"How do you bathe in that icehouse? I ask out of a genuine thirst for knowledge, you understand. Nothing prurient intended."

"Quickly," she said shortly, standing up and collecting her dishes.

"You're always in a hurry, aren't you?" Luke sat down and peered doubtfully at the oatmeal, fixed himself a cup of coffee with milk, and reached automatically for his cigarettes. He then grimaced and put them back. "What's on your busy schedule for today?"

"Fence mending," Delilah told him. She was already reaching for her windbreaker. She wouldn't need the cap and vest this morning. The sun was shining, and although the icy wind off the snowy upper slopes would make her face and ears ache, she knew she would be exercising hard enough to keep warm. "Before lambing starts I want to be sure there aren't any holes in my pasture fences that coyotes can get through. Last year I lost several of my best lambs, and I can't afford to let that happen again."

Luke drained his coffee cup and stood up. "Mind if I come along? I need to take a look at my plane anyway."

She paused. "Are you sure you're up to it? Shouldn't you . . . eat something?"

He glanced at the cold oatmeal and smiled slightly. "Maybe later."

She shrugged. "Well, suit yourself. Um . . . would you please put that oatmeal in the refrigerator if you're not going to eat it?"

"Glad to," he said cheerfully. "Mind if I ask what you intend to do with it?"

"Eat it," she replied succinctly, glancing at him in surprise.

He repressed a shudder. "You don't eat—you refuel."

"I do what I have to do," she retorted, bristling instantly at the implied criticism. "And I get along just *fine.*"

"Um-hmm. Obviously a strong, independent woman of few words and simple tastes." His voice was softly teasing. It prodded the embers of her anger in ways she couldn't understand. She only knew that every time his voice took on that certain timbre, every time his eyes smiled at her with that certain warmth, she felt . . . besieged.

"That's me," she said staunchly, with an involuntary lift of her chin, "strong and independent."

Luke chuckled. "Hardy pioneer stock."

"*My* ancestors," Delilah retorted haughtily, "were more likely to be attacking covered wagons than riding in them."

"Really?" His eyebrows lifted in surprise.

"Well, some of them," she admitted, smiling wryly. Odd, she mused, the way her anger evaporated the minute he turned off those magnetic charms of his. "My mother's grandmother was full-blooded Navaho."

"Ah, I see." Luke was studying her with keen interest. "Are your folks in the sheep business too?"

"You mean, am I carrying on an old Navaho tradition?"

"I noticed the loom. Did you make the rugs yourself?"

"Some of them. My grandmother taught me to weave." She followed his gaze as it swept over the richly patterned rugs that made her home so cozy, warming almost against her will to the genuine interest in his eyes. "My . . . mother died when I was very small," she offered. "My father is a judge."

"A judge!" A peculiar look crossed Luke MacGregor's expressive face. "I don't believe it," he muttered, and Delilah hastened to assure him that her father had trouble believing it himself, at times.

Luke looked at her without comprehension and mumbled, "What?" as if he had been thinking of something else. It seemed to Delilah that they had diverged at some point in this conversation and were now headed in completely different directions.

"Yes . . . well," she murmured in confusion, frowning at the soft pullover that molded to his slender body like a second skin. "Your jacket is still damp, and I don't have anything—"

"I'll find something in the plane. Don't worry about it," he said briskly, sounding like a different person entirely. For the first time, he seemed like someone who might have founded a corporation. "I'm ready—let's go."

After a brief stop at the haystack to collect wire cutters and an armload of baling wire, they walked together up the slope to the pasture, following the same path they had come down the evening before. Now, though, the sun was shining, the sky was a brilliant blue filled with scudding, windblown clouds, and there was no trace of the snow that had fallen steadily the day before. Even the moisture had evaporated in the dry, desert air or soaked into the porous, gravelly soil. The air was clean and sweet, with a bite that suggested not-too-distant peaks where the snows never melted.

They separated at the gate, Luke angling across the middle of the pasture to where the orange plane sat giddily askew, a giant, broken dragonfly. Delilah began her slow circumnavigation, kneeling now and then to check the soundness of the fence fabric and pausing to watch Luke's progress. Last night he had leaned heavily on her, his knees weakened by shock, but even then she had guessed he would be graceful. His was a natural, unconscious grace. He had the symmetry of a wild animal and was completely comfortable with his body, aware of its limitations as well as its capabilities. He walked easily, head up, hands tucked in his hip pockets, the wind catching at his longish hair and lifting it away from the sculptured bones of his face. He didn't seem to feel the cold wind that must have been penetrating the thin pullover like needles. Delilah watched him stop and study the crippled plane, run a hand along the sloping wing, and then pull himself into the cockpit with one easy, fluid motion. She pressed her lips firmly together, shifted her armload of wire, and plodded on, following the fence.

The cockpit was eerily quiet. Luke eased himself into the pilot's seat, bracing himself against the cant of the floor, and waited for a cold chill to slither along the length of his spine. He reached for the cigarettes he kept behind the seat, lit one, and inhaled deeply and luxuriously. Close, Mac, he told himself with a mental whistle. Too damn close. He thoughtfully fingered the neat dental-floss stitchery in his scalp and began experimentally pushing buttons. Something in the electrical system, he thought. Shouldn't be too difficult to pinpoint. That and the landing gear. With some welding equipment he could have the plane ready to fly again in no time at all. The trick would be to get it airborne from this pasture. He was no stunt pilot.

He gave his head a somber shake and reached for the phone. In a few minutes he had raised the mobile operator and was putting a call through to Mammoth.

"Mac! Hey, old buddy—" Pete's thin, distant voice cracked, and there was a slight pause. "Hey, how the hell are you? *Where* the hell are you?"

Luke chuckled and settled back, amazed at the sting of emotion behind his own eyes. "I'm fine, Pete. Just fine. You wouldn't believe it. Call it the luck of the MacGregors, I guess."

"Well, where are you? We got the call from the county mounties last night, but all they said was that you had made, quote, a successful emergency landing, end quote, and were okay. Why in hell didn't you call?"

"I didn't call because I was out cold—"

"What?"

"—and because this pasture doesn't have a phone. At least it didn't until I put one in it. I'm calling from the plane."

"You're kidding. You spent the night in the plane?"

Luke laughed. "Hardly. Listen, it's a long story. I'll tell you all about it when I see you. Any news?"

"Yeah. Good and bad. The bad news is, no dice on getting the drilling moratorium lifted. The good news is, we've finally got a hearing date—April seventeenth. Now, if we could just get a change of venue, or at least a different judge, we might have a chance. The way I see it, with Beaumont presiding again we might just as well pack it in."

"Maybe . . ." Luke said slowly. "Maybe not. Do me a favor, will you, Pete?"

"Another one? By the way, I hope you didn't wipe out any sheep. Our policy doesn't include sheep-collision insurance."

"Forget the blasted sheep. Just find out if Judge Beaumont has a daughter, will you?"

"Right . . . A *what*?"

"Daughter. As in female offspring."

"Gotcha. I think. What do I do when I find out?"

"Sit tight. I'll be in touch."

"Okay. Oh, by the way, Glenna says to tell you she's put away a bottle of champagne, and John saved the garter for you. He says he doesn't know anybody who deserves it more."

Luke grinned. "Fat chance. So long, Pete. I'll be talking to you."

He cradled the receiver and sat a few minutes longer, smoking and thoughtfully watching a small dark-haired figure in a red windbreaker clumping along the fence line in heavy rubber boots.

An hour later Delilah was teetering on the next-to-last rung of a very old, very weathered wooden stepladder, her shins braced against the flat top step more for reassurance than for balance. She was trying to screw a large steel hook into the two-by-four that ran around the top of the outer cement block barn wall, under the eaves. It was proving unexpectedly difficult. Perspiration kept trickling into her eyes, stinging just enough to add one more aggravation to her general discomfort and irritability.

She was out of sorts and depressed, for reasons she couldn't even begin to understand. Was it anger toward Luke MacGregor she was feeling, or was it fear? Fear of failure, maybe? Or fear that it wasn't going to be worth it after all—that she would wake up some morning and find that she'd been chasing the wrong rainbow? . . .

"What are you doing now?"

The voice from below shot through her like a bolt of electricity, startling her so badly that she tottered and clutched wildly at the roof's overhang.

"Lord . . ." she muttered under her breath, and closed her eyes briefly. "Don't sneak up on a person standing on a ladder!" she said sternly, looking down at him.

"Sorry. I didn't know I was sneaking. I made enough noise, but you must have been a million miles away. What were you thinking about?" His smile was gentle, almost seductive. Habit, probably, she thought, and damned unnerving in the middle of a bright and windy March morning. Or *was* it still morning? Her stomach had begun to churn again. She pressed her fingers to her lips and cleared her throat.

"I was trying," she said carefully, "to think of a way to get electricity into this barn." She gave the hook another quarter turn, then abandoned the effort and turned around to sit on the top of the ladder, hugging her knees to her chest. Looking down at him from this height made her feel safer . . . and also made her conscious of her vulnerability.

His smile had slipped sideways into a wry grin, almost as if he were following her train of thought. Delilah gave herself a vigorous mental shake and started warily down the ladder. To her great relief, Luke stayed where he was, a few feet away, his arms crossed on his chest, not moving to steady the ladder for her descent.

"I'm curious," he said when she was back on solid footing, both physically and emotionally. "Why do you want electricity in a barn, when you don't even have heat in your bathroom?"

"It's my lambing barn," she explained, brushing splinters out of the seat of her pants. "It's hard to hold a flashlight and assist a ewe in labor at the same time. I could also use a heatlamp to dry the lambs. The weaker ones can get chilled on especially cold nights."

"I would have thought lambs were bred for that sort of weather," Luke commented. "Whereas you weren't. Don't *you* get cold?"

"I'm not generally wet. You'd be surprised at how much moisture a coat of lamb's wool can hold. And you'd be surprised how warm a barn full of sheep can get. Even with the windows open on the coldest nights it can be like a sauna. That's another reason I'd like electricity—I'd install a fan to circulate the air."

"Sounds like your sheep will have it better than you do," he said dryly. "Can I see inside?"

"Sure," she said, and gave him a skeptical, sideways glance, wondering what interest a corporation president could possibly have in her barn. When she looked at him, though, her breath got hung up in her throat. Darn, she thought. It wasn't only a beautiful face, it was a *nice* face, reflecting only cheery curiosity. She cleared her throat and muttered, "Be my guest."

She opened the door and waved him inside. He stopped beside her and his brown eyes subtly changed shape, becoming lethal, black-fringed weapons again. His hand touched the side of her head briefly, almost casually, the tips of his fingers threading through her hair, the heel of his hand resting at the hinge of her jaw. Then he smiled and moved on past her, and strolled down the wide center aisle between rows of stalls, hands in hip pockets, taking in everything with his sweeping, interested glance.

Delilah followed, answering questions without self-consciousness. She was proud of her barn. She'd designed it herself, and even if she hadn't been able to afford the luxuries of running water and electricity, it was built to suit her specifications.

"Twenty stalls," Luke observed. "You said you have ninety-some-odd ewes. How do you manage?"

"Well, they won't all lamb at once," she said dryly. "I only have three rams. It would be physically impossible."

"Oops." Luke chuckled. "You can tell I'm not a farm boy." He turned away, frowning up at the rafters. "Just how do you propose to bring in electricity, by the way?"

"Nothing fancy. I mean to run a heavy-duty extension cord from the house. I . . . haven't figured out exactly *how*, yet, but I've still got a week to work it out."

Luke squinted thoughtfully at her and said, "Uh-huh." He moved on down the center aisle to the door at the far end, opened it for an investigative look, then pushed it wide and stood in the doorway gazing out. Delilah knew that vista—it was her favorite. Beyond the pinkish-gray skeletons of the apple trees was the pale greenish brown of the winter pasture, and beyond that the dun-colored hills, just showing the green of new grass and dotted with juniper, sage, and yucca. And the most breathtaking sight of all, the ice-blue backdrop of the Sierras, the eastern escarpment that rises sharply from below sea level to some of the highest peaks on the continent. The sight of her flock grazing peacefully in its shadow never failed to give Delilah's heart a lift.

"I guess the fattest ones are the most pregnant," Luke said.

"Not necessarily. Looks can be deceiving. Some may be carrying twins or triplets, and some just . . . get bigger than others."

"Then, how do you tell when it's time to bring them into the barn? I don't suppose they tell you."

"I keep records, of course," Delilah said, realizing that the conversation was going to take a rather embarrassing turn, but not knowing how to divert it. "Breeding records. So I know within a few days when a ewe is due to lamb. But the most reliable method is to check . . . um, udder development."

"I see," Luke said, absolutely straight-faced. "And how do you accomplish *that*?"

She drew in a deep gulp of sage-scented air. "As a matter of fact, it needs to be done now. But I thought you needed to get to a telephone. Don't you want—"

"I'm in no hurry." He tucked his hands in his hip pockets and grinned. "I wouldn't miss this for anything."

"What about lunch? You didn't eat breakfast. Don't you—"

"I went in and made myself a sandwich while you were fixing the fence. I hope it was all right—I didn't want to trouble you. I found what was left of a chicken."

"Umpf," Delilah mumbled. That chicken would have made two meals for her. "All right," she said with resignation. "I'll get them into the pen."

As she poured grain in a long, thin trail the entire length of the four wooden troughs in the holding pen, she gave her long, high call. Immediately Lady appeared from nowhere and went streaking off across the pasture. Imperious black heads were lifted and a general stampede toward the pen began, encouraged and controlled by the scurrying little tricolored dog.

As the flock thundered through the gate and spread out along the troughs, Delilah was busy unrolling a length of wire fence-fabric across the end of the pen closest to the pasture. She wired the gate shut with a length of baling wire. There were now about twenty animals in this smaller enclosure. She walked slowly through the busily masticating sheep, checking numbers painted on woolly backs, glancing at numbered and colored ear tags. Singling out one ewe she knew should be among the first to lamb, she hooked an arm across and under the animal's neck and grabbed the hard bony black head with her other hand, forcing the nose up. The ewe's angry bolt carried them both a few feet before Delilah managed to brace herself and pull the black nose even higher. Now she could control the direction of the ewe's flight, and she wrestled her up broadside against the fence, pinning her there with a knee against her flank. Using the whole weight of her body to hold the animal, she leaned sideways, still keeping one arm around the ewe's neck, and reached back under the round belly to the smaller roundness between the hind legs. A moment later she stepped away, and the ewe dashed back to the trough.

Delilah turned, only slightly out of breath, to find Luke watching her with something very close to horror. She felt an unexpected surge of exhilaration.

He coughed and shook his head. "And you go through that . . . ninety-five times?"

"Oh," Delilah said blithely, waving her hand, "not all at once. I only check the ones I know are close to lambing." She was showing off—blatantly. And it was *fun.*

"Can I help?"

She laughed with sheer delight. "Be my guest! Uh . . . that one there, with the blue ear tag. Number 907." Number 907 was a big purebred Suffolk two-year-old, and this was her first lambing. She wasn't used to being handled. Delilah folded her arms on her chest and watched with gleeful anticipation as the president of Thermodyne stepped confidently up to the ewe and placed his arms around the woolly neck.

"Better get her nose up," Delilah said helpfully, but of course it was already too late. Number 907 had put her head down and was charging full-tilt across the pen. Luke swore violently and briefly, and let go. He came hobbling back to the fence, muttering under his breath.

"Damn thing stepped on my foot!" he said with a growl, glaring accusingly at Delilah. "What was that, a renegade? I can't believe you can handle that animal."

Delilah, enjoying herself hugely, calmly stepped into the milling flock, corraled number 907, and pinned her against the fence. After checking her udder, Delilah released her and smiled up at Luke's incredulous face.

"It isn't a matter of strength," she said soothingly. "It would take a bulldogger to stop a Suffolk with its head down. The trick is to get the nose *up.* That way the sheep can't get any momentum, and probably can't see where it's going, either."

"Well," Luke grumbled, nursing his bruised instep and a more severely battered ego, "this seems like an unnecessary amount of trouble to go through for animals that are supposed to run loose out on the range, holding their own against weather and predators. I can't believe real sheepmen nursemaid their flocks with custom-built maternity wards."

Delilah felt herself go rigid with anger. "I assure you I am a 'real sheepman,' " she said coldly. "I just can't afford the thirty-to-fifty-percent lamb mortality rate you can expect under range conditions. Excuse me."

As she opened the gate to let the sheep in the partitioned enclosure back out into the pasture, she was conscious not only of anger, but of bitter disappointment. So, she thought, for all his charm he was no different from any other man. They were ready with smiles and kisses just as long as their precious egos remained unthreatened, as long as a woman looked harmless and helpless. But just let them meet up with a woman whose knowledge and expertise was superior to theirs in one of their male-dominated fields, and bingo! It was attack, no holds barred. Damn, they were all alike.

"Finished already?" Luke asked as Delilah began rolling up the makeshift partition.

"I'll do it tomorrow," she replied shortly and pointedly. "When I have more time. I'm sure you're eager to get to a telephone."

He opened his mouth and closed it again, looking strangely guilty. She wondered briefly what he had meant to say, then put it out of her mind. It had nothing at all to do with her—and the sooner she got rid of him, the better.

"Can I ask you a question?" he asked suddenly as they walked back through the orchard. His hands were tucked in his pockets and he limped slightly, frowning down at his feet as they wove through winter-bare trees. "Why did you choose to get into this—sheep-ranching?"

"Why do you do whatever it is you do?" she returned sharply.

He gave her a quick, hard look. "My dad was an Oklahoma wildcatter. I have degrees in geology and engineering. Exploring alternative sources of energy is a new and exciting frontier. *My* choice of careers makes sense; yours doesn't. What is it—some kind of rebellion? You have something to prove?"

Delilah corraled her temper, wrestling it the way she did an obstreperous ewe. "Maybe," she said evenly. "Maybe I just need to prove that *I* can do what I've always dreamed of doing, the same as any man. Raising sheep may be an occupation as old as civilization, but it's every bit as challenging and exciting as poking holes in the planet's crust! It makes sense to be doing what I'm doing, because it's what I *want* to do. Does *that* answer your question?" She had not, of course, been able to maintain that hold on her temper. It had put its nose down and gotten right away from her. She stopped walking and faced Luke, chest heaving, while he gazed stonily down at her, his mouth twisted in a humorless smile.

"Partly," he said quietly, his calm making Delilah feel churlish and foolish. "But why alone? And why sheep? They seem to be almost more trouble than they're worth."

"I'm alone," she said, struggling to match his self-possession, "because I don't want partners and can't afford help. And I chose sheep because I can handle them alone. Physically. Cattle require horses, or the modern equivalent; manpower, strength. All I need is my dog. To assist a laboring cow in trouble requires a special chute, block and tackle, and great big muscles. And then it's usually not successful. With sheep, I can single-handedly deliver a tangled-up set of triplets. Successfully."

"I've seen the way you handle your sheep," Luke said dryly. "You don't have to convince me. *That* part I can understand." He left the comment unfinished, and turned his head to study the three rams in the small enclosure at his elbow. The biggest of them, a huge gray-muzzled Suffolk with a Roman nose and legs like tree limbs, faced them suspiciously and stamped a warning. Luke jerked his thumb in that direction, his eyes glittering. "You 'handle' him too?"

"No," Delilah retorted. "Those are the rams. Like all males, they do pretty much as they please."

Before she stalked off and left Luke standing there, she saw his mouth tighten and his eyes narrow. About halfway to the house it occurred to her that he was actually angry, as she had been. Was still. And it struck her like a blow to the solar plexus that people did not go around having quarrels with casual strangers. Somehow the fact that she had quarreled with Luke MacGregor gave her more of a sense of intimate violation than anything that had happened up to now. Including the strange good-morning kiss. In less than twenty-four hours that man had managed to get under her skin in a way no human being ever had before. If it were not for the fact that he would be leaving soon, very probably for good, she would be terrified. So why didn't that thought make her feel better?

While Delilah was in the house, Luke put another call through to Pete.

"Mac!" Pete said. "Glad you called. Perfect timing."

"What've you got?" Luke asked as he lit a cigarette.

"Well, I don't know how you knew, but Beaumont does have a daughter. Vitals: Age, twenty-five, brown hair, blue eyes, five feet two, hundred and ten pounds. That sound right so far?"

"To a point," Luke said dryly. "Anything else?"

"Yeah . . . let's see. Degrees from Cal Poly and U.C. Davis. No record, not even a parking ticket. But a friend of mine in Sacramento tells me the kid is something of a black sheep. Didn't say why . . . What's funny?"

"Funny you should mention sheep. You'll never believe whose pasture I'm sitting in."

"I give up, whose?"

"Don't be dense, Pete."

"You're kidding."

"No, I'm not."

"Delilah Beaumont raises *sheep*?"

"Yup. She owns this place—bought it outright with some federal Indian money. Did you know Beaumont's wife was a quarter Navaho?"

"No kiddin'. Mac, you realize we may have something here? This could be the break we need."

"I thought of that. We might be able to charge bias, with a member of the judge's immediate family owning property here, but it's shaky."

"Yeah. Hey, I don't suppose there's any way you could marry this chick between now and the seventeenth. I know it's short notice, but I've seen the way you operate. Maybe—"

"Forget it. This girl has something against men. She's got a thing about her independence—you know, the fem-lib thing. Headstrong as the devil."

"Sounds like a chip off the old bench to me. Well, we'll do what we can with this property angle. When you are comin' home, old buddy?"

Luke was staring through the windshield, his eyes squinted thoughtfully against the sting of cigarette smoke. "How are you doing up there?" he asked casually. "Holding down the fort okay?"

"Shoot, man, we're a ghost town around here, with that drilling moratorium in effect. Angie mans the phone and does her nails, and I hang around just to keep up appearances. Why?"

"Oh, I thought I might take a little leave of absence."

"Mac." The grin came over the wire as vividly as if it had been a video feed. "You got something in mind?"

"Let's say I have an idea that might keep me around here for a while longer. Never can tell what kind of useful information might turn up."

"Well, I sure wish you luck. We need a bit. Hey—you take care of yourself, you hear? That girl's got the blood of Indians and French-Canadian trappers in her veins. You could wake up without your scalp. Now what's funny?"

Luke fingered the stitches in his head. "She's already had her chance at my scalp."

"Remember what happened to Samson!"

Delilah was standing over the sink, sullenly eating

cold oatmeal straight from the pot, when Luke came in carrying a flight bag, a zippered plastic suit bag slung over his shoulder. He gave her a quizzical look and she glared back at him over the pot, daring him to make a remark about her eating habits. But he only gestured toward the bathroom with the suit bag and said politely, "May I?"

"Be my guest." She waved her spoon with what she knew was a deplorable lack of grace, considering who he was and his reason for being in her house.

She had put the pot in the sink and filled it with water, and was on her way to her bedroom to change her clothes, when she heard a car drive up. She turned back, to peer out the window. "Oh, *damn,*" she muttered, feeling the ominous weight of what could very well be the last straw.

"Hello, Amos," she said without warmth as she opened the door to her neighbor, adding with blatant insincerity, "How nice to see you."

Subtlety was wasted on Amos Chappel. The rancher had always reminded Delilah of John Wayne—with all of the mannerisms and none of the charm. He walked with the same bent-forward-at-the-hips, rolling-sideways swagger, the result of having spent too much of his youth with his legs curled around bucking livestock. He was a rancher of the old school. He figured women somewhere just above a good cow and just below a good cutting horse in value and importance. And, with the possible exception of country singers and rodeo groupies, he firmly believed that a woman's place was in the kitchen. Needless to say, he and Delilah hadn't hit it off.

If basic philosophy had been the only difference between them, there probably wouldn't have been a problem. Although Amos was her nearest neighbor, their property lines didn't actually adjoin. The problem stemmed from a century-old homestead grant that gave to the owner of Delilah's property sole water rights to a creek that flowed down from the Sierra snowpack.

Amos had tried to buy the place from Delilah, offering

half again what she'd paid for it. When that failed, he'd tried to buy the water rights themselves, claiming that Delilah couldn't possibly need all that water for such a little bunch of sheep. But his latest idea was by far the most irksome. Having failed to acquire the land or the water, he was now embarked on a determined campaign to acquire Delilah . . . and was proving unexpectedly hard to discourage.

"Delilah, honey," he drawled by way of a greeting, taking off his hat and resting it and his hand on his hip. He gripped the back of a chair with the other hand and leaned toward her. "You know, darned if you don't get prettier every time I see you!"

Delilah glanced down at her baggy, grubby sweat shirt and faded jeans. "Thanks," she said dryly.

"Shoot, I darn near forgot why I come. I was downtown this mornin', and I heard about that plane puttin' down in your pasture. I see that plane still up there, and I see it's done some damage, too. Now, I was thinkin', Delilah, honey, gettin' that pile of junk outa there is goin' to be a bigger job than I reckon you can handle. Now, with my A-frame and my flatbed—"

"Amos. That plane is not my concern. It is up to the person who put it there to take it out. Personally, I don't intend to let it worry me."

"Well, now," Amos went on good-naturedly, "that's true enough. But you want to be careful of these big ol' corporations, you know. They'd be apt to take advantage of a little bitty gal like yourself, honey. They got their insurance and their tax shelters. Well, shoot, they'll probably declare it a total loss and leave it lay."

"If they do," Delilah said airily, "I'll use it for a hay manger. Look, Amos—"

She broke off as he rested a big brown hand on each of her shoulders and squinted down at her in a superior way. "Hon, now, are you gonna go and be bullheaded about this? I can have my boys over here tomorrow, have that contraption out of your hair in no time at all."

"Thank you, Amos, but no," Delilah said firmly. His

cowboy hat was tickling the back of her neck. "I don't want—"

"Damned if you ain't the proudest little thing I ever saw!" Amos gave his head a shake and grinned. "But come on, now, hon, this here's ol' Amos talkin'. You don't need to get up on that high horse with me, 'cause I know you ain't got a nickel to spare and more work'n you can handle. Shoot, honey, why don't you quit bein' so doggone stubborn and give up this whole damn-fool sheep idea and marry me? There ain't no money in sheep, and this little ol' place ain't big enough to support a jackrabbit anyhow. Now, I got a real nice spread, Delilah, you know that. You can have just about anything you want."

"What I want," said Delilah through her teeth, "is to raise my sheep on my own place. And for you to leave me alone."

The rancher's prominent jaw tightened, and his eyes narrowed. "Boy, for pure cussedness, you take the cake. Damnation, gal, it seems to me somebody shoulda taken you in hand a long time ago!"

Delilah felt his hands tighten on her shoulders and read his intent. She braced herself, her hands coming up to ward him off, and ducked her head to avoid his kiss.

The quiet voice was a shock to both of them. "What's going on?" Luke MacGregor asked.

Four

Amos dropped his hands and turned to stare. Over his shoulder Delilah could see a pair of black-fringed eyes, which at the moment were as hard and cold as marbles. When Amos moved so that she could see the rest of that handsome face, she was startled to see a pleasant smile on the lower half of it.

"Luke," she said faintly, aware of an unusual warmth in her cheeks.

"Any problem, darling?"

Darling?

Luke was leveling that curiously flat stare at Amos, who was looking more than usually mulish. Delilah shook her head, unable to think of a thing to say. She moved away from Amos and was shocked speechless when Luke added in a voice husky with implied intimacy, "Come help me with this collar button, will you, love?"

Love?

He was wearing a fawn-colored suede sport jacket, dark slacks, and a textured silk shirt. Locks of his hair, damp around the edges, fell silkily forward as he bent toward her. He lifted his chin to give her clear access to his throat and tugged with exasperated ineffectiveness at his collar. He smiled at her with heart-stopping radiance. "For some reason it keeps eluding me." And he winked.

Delilah drew in her breath in a desperate gulp and reached toward his snowy-white shirtfront, appalled to see that her hands were shaking. Behind her she heard Amos ask belligerently, "Hey, who the hell is this guy?"

"Oh, sorry," Luke said. "MacGregor. Luke Mac-Gregor." He grinned pleasantly and reached around Delilah to offer his hand. "That's my plane out there. Don't know what I'd have done if that pasture hadn't been there." He turned that potent dark gaze on Delilah even as Amos absentmindedly and uncertainly pumped the proffered hand. Delilah, thus enclosed in fawn suede and enveloped in a subtle aura of after-shave and shower-heated male, promptly forgot how to breathe.

"Surprised you're still around," Amos muttered gruffly.

"Yeah . . . well," Luke murmured. Delilah, the top of her head just about even with his mouth, could feel the warm puff of his soft laughter.

What *was* he doing? she wondered. Biting fiercely at her lower lip, she slipped her fingers inside his collar and drew the two ends together. His skin was moist and very warm. His pulse hammered against the backs of her fingers, an insistent rhythm that seemed to flow down her arms and into her body, taking over and dominating her own frantic cadence.

"Turned out to be kind of hard to leave, didn't it, baby?" he said.

Baby?

Somehow, miraculously, Delilah got that button fastened. She stood back, winded and glaring. Luke bent his head and gave her a lingering kiss. "Thanks, babe. I'll be ready in a minute. I'll just get the rest of my things out of the bedroom. . . ." He gave her another eye-crinkling smile that melted her bones, and turned away. About halfway to the bedroom he stopped and turned. "Oh—nice to have met you . . . I don't believe I caught your name."

"Amos Chappel," Delilah said hoarsely. "My neighbor."

"Ah. Mr. Chappel. Well, nice meeting you. That's one terrific neighbor you've got here." He grinned one last time and went on into the bedroom. Delilah could hear him whistling beyond the closed door.

She turned slowly back to Amos, not at all surprised to find that his eyes were slits and his lips a thin line of contempt. "Amos," she began, knowing there was really nothing she particularly wanted to say.

"Delilah," Amos said, breathing heavily through his nose, "are you telling me that—that fella spent the night here with you last night?"

"Yes," she said, "I guess he did." The seeds of mirth were sprouting deep inside her. She tried halfheartedly to stunt them.

"In your *bed?*"

"That's right." With great effort she kept her face solemn.

"A *stranger?*" Amos was almost sputtering. It struck Delilah so funny that all she could do without bursting into guffaws of laughter was lift her shoulders in a helpless shrug. Behind her she heard the bedroom door open.

"Delilah," Amos said, shaking his head sorrowfully, "I'd'a thought a lot of things about you, some good and some bad, but I always figured with a little straightenin' out—a firm hand—you'd make a pretty decent wife. I sure never figured you for a . . . a . . ." He struggled for a word, frowning down at the hat he was turning over and over in his hands. Finally, almost triumphantly, he spat out, ". . . a *strumpet!*"

Delilah smothered a desperate gust of laughter only by clamping the tips of her fingers over her mouth. Amos gave her a fearsome scowl, clamped his hat down on his head, and stomped out. When the door slammed, Delilah folded her arms across her stomach and doubled over, helpless with laughter, unable to make a sound.

From behind, Luke took her by the arms and turned

her. "Delilah?" His voice sounded puzzled, almost fearful.

"Oh," she gasped, clutching at the soft suede lapels. "Oh, Luke. I can't . . . believe . . . you did that!" Tears were streaming down her face, and she struggled for breath. "Poor Amos."

"Delilah . . . Look, I'm sorry. I thought—"

"*Sorry*? Did you hear what he . . . what he called me? A *strumpet!*" And now at last a howl of laughter escaped her. She whooped and chortled helplessly into Luke's shirtfront, only dimly aware that his body had relaxed, that his arms had gone around her, and that his hands were stroking her back. . . .

Gradually her laughter died into fitful giggles and contented sighs. She felt so *good*, happy and relaxed, utterly at peace, without a care in the world. Her cheek was pillowed on Luke's chest, her head fitting perfectly under his chin. Her arms were around his waist, inside his jacket, the warmth of his body pervasive and intimate. His hands . . . His hands were roaming sensuously over her back, triggering involuntary cuddle responses. She moved against him like a cat being petted.

Awareness came simultaneously to them both, with different effects. Luke's hands slipped down, past her waist, to the taut curve of her bottom, and his body tensed and tightened. Delilah's tensed too. She stiffened and pushed away from him, whispered, "Oh, Lord," and sank into a chair.

For a few moments there was silence; then Luke sat down across the table from her and reached for a cigarette. "You had me worried there for a minute." His voice was casual, amused. "I thought I'd misread the whole situation when you doubled up like that."

He was releasing her, letting her off the hook, she realized, watching his hands as he tapped out a cigarette, paused, then put the pack away. She was grateful for his chivalry, but still couldn't bring herself to look at him. "Do you know," she murmured unsteadily, "that in a matter of seconds you managed to do what I've been trying to do for two solid years? Do you have any idea how hard it is to discourage that man?" She put her face in her hands, overcome by a fit of giggles that was half residual amusement and half nervous tension. "*Strumpet.* Oh, my." She sighed, exhausted, and finally dared to lift her gaze to Luke's face.

My goodness, but he was gorgeous, she thought. He had put on a tie in the bedroom, a dark brown knit that matched his hair and eyes. Against the snowy white of his shirt his skin had a dusky matte texture, his hair a satin sheen. His eyes, without the charismatic twinkle, held hers in a long, sober look. He was so wonderful to look at, she wanted to go on doing it forever. And so, perversely, she turned away, refusing to allow herself to look at him at all.

Deep, deep inside her, in the secret hideaway of her emotions, something was aborning. What a temptation it would be to nurture it, she thought, and let it grow. . . .

"Delilah—"

"I'll change my clothes," she said huskily, struggling to rise. "I know you'd like to get out of here."

His hand reached for hers, but he didn't touch her. She looked at him, half-fearful. "What?" she asked.

"Please." His eyes looked almost black. She settled slowly back in her chair. "Listen to me for a minute, all right? Hear me out before you start arguing."

She stared at him without comprehension, and he took a deep breath. "I have a proposition for you. How would you like a hired hand? For the duration of your lambing season, room and board, no strings attached?"

It seemed like a very long time before Delilah could think of anything to say. He might have been speaking Swahili, for all the sense his words made to her. Finally she decided he must be making some sort of obscure joke.

"Um-hm, I'd like that," she said, beginning to nod. "And then I'd like to win a sweepstakes and be a five-foot-seven blonde." She managed a dry sound that was only half laughter.

Luke's hand moved toward hers again. "I'm serious."

"You're serious." Now anger became an ingredient in her confusion. She snatched her hand out of danger and stood up. "That's just great. What did you do—get rid of Amos just so you could take his place?"

"Look, I don't know what you're talking about. I didn't mean to make you mad—"

"Mad? Me? I never get mad." She had started for the sink, but now returned to clutch at the back of a chair. With icy control she said, "What I really am is curious. That man who just left here has been trying for two solid years to worm his way into control of this place by offering me free hired help—free this, free that. I thought his price was too high. Now I'm wondering what *your* price is. What do you want from me? Are you going to tell me there's natural gas under my land? Hot water, maybe?"

"What an interesting possibility," Luke said in the same mildly reproving manner that had made her feel so childish this morning. "I'll look into it."

"Over my dead body." She straightened and sniffed. "I don't need your hired hand any more than I need Amos's."

"Or any more than you need legs," Luke said quietly. He leaned back in his chair and regarded her steadily. A slight smile played about his mouth. "But I don't think you understand. I'm not trying to give you a hired hand. I'm offering to work for you."

Seconds ticked slowly by, uncounted. Delilah lowered herself carefully into the chair and placed her hands palms down on the oilcloth. She felt a giddy urge to laugh. "Um, excuse me. You're telling me you want to work for me? For nothing?"

"Not for nothing. For room and board."

"One of us," she said crisply, "is losing his mind." Suddenly he moved, shifted in his chair, and it was as if he'd released a charge of pure animal magnetism. The air crackled with it, and Delilah found herself staring at the knot of his tie and remembering with full sensual recall the feel of his warm neck against the backs of her fingers. Dragging her gaze away with an effort of will, she gave a dismissive sniff and said lightly, "Well, I'm sorry, but I seriously doubt that you're qualified for the job anyway."

"Oh, yeah?" His eyes smiled at her, quietly confident. "What makes you think that?"

You're too beautiful, she wanted to say. You smell too good. You make me feel like Annie Oakley.

Instead she snorted. "Oh, for heaven's sake, be serious. Talk about overqualified! And just look at yourself. Sheep ranching's hard, dirty work."

"Don't let the tie fool you," Luke drawled, his eyes glittering. "I've worked oil rigs since I was nine."

"What about recently?" she muttered doubtfully, adding, "You told me you were a city boy."

"I'm a fast learner." He shifted again, becoming placating, as though she were an intractable child. "Look, Delilah. What's the problem? You need help . . . and I owe you."

"Oh, no. No." She stood up with an angry gesture. "Look, Mr. MacGregor," she said, emphasizing his name, reminding them both of who he was and where he really belonged. As she began to pace, rubbing defensively at her arms, her reactions zigzagged from anger to disbelief, and finally to unease. He seemed serious, so either he was completely crazy or he wanted something from her. But what? What could a stranded executive, a man she'd never heard of before in her life, possibly want from her? She took a deep breath, preparing to be reasonable. "I don't mean to be rude, but you have to admit that you sound . . . a little crazy. You are an executive, aren't you? You're so busy you fly your own plane to get where you want to go, and yet you crash-land in my pasture and the next day offer to work off the damage personally? I'm sorry, but I know executives. If you thought you owed me anything you'd offer to pay me off, not work. Executives value their time above anything in the world."

Luke laughed good-naturedly. "Well, that's true enough, unless the executive happens to have more time than money." It was as if someone had activated a dimmer switch, Delilah thought. Although he was smiling, the laughter didn't touch his eyes. "I'm . . . having a little trouble with the courts. My company's temporarily shut down. A little forced vacation, you might say."

"Oh, come on," she snapped. "And there's nothing in the world you'd rather do with your vacation than herd sheep? You live in Mammoth, right? Maybe you hadn't noticed, but the skiing isn't too shabby up there this time of year. Or wait—maybe the bright lights are more your style. Reno's just a short airplane ride over the mountain. And, for that matter, where were you going when you crashed? You must have had something—"

"How'd you get to be so damn cynical?" Luke exploded, then reined himself in with visible effort. "Look, I don't understand the third degree. You're looking a pretty good gift horse in the mouth, it seems to me. You have a big problem here, and I thought—"

"You thought I'd jump at the offer?" Delilah paused in front of him, incredulous. "Mr. MacGregor, I don't know you from Adam. I've known you less than a day, and your story is, excuse me, more than a tad farfetched! I just can't buy it, and I can't figure out what you really want from me, and that makes me very nervous!"

Luke smiled at her, and his voice acquired those husky, spine-tingling dissonances. "Would you believe I fell madly in love with you at first sight and just want to be near you?"

"No," Delilah said, unmoved. "I wouldn't."

He hesitated just long enough, allowed his gaze to become just intense enough, to start a shiver on its way down her spine. Then he gave a shrug that seemed to say, "It was worth a try," and said blandly, "I'll bet you'd believe me if I said I just wanted to jump on your bones."

She managed to keep her voice at the opposite end of the temperature scale from her temper. "I wouldn't believe that either."

With real curiosity he asked, "Why not?"

"I'm sure you don't have to go this far to find a presentable set of bones, Mr. MacGregor," she said dryly.

"Cut the 'Mister' stuff. My name is Luke." He had a stubborn, implacable look—the look of a man bent on getting what he wanted. It occurred to Delilah that there might be a darker side to the charming Luke Mac-Gregor, even a ruthless side. He started to rake his fingers through his hair, encountered his injury, winced, and made an impatient gesture with his hand. "I'd just like to stick around for a while, that's all. I thought I could pay my way and help you out at the same time."

He got up from the table and strolled to the window. Again he touched the wound in his scalp, then dropped his hand to his side. Every move he made was graceful, Delilah thought, watching the pull of expensive fabric across his shoulders. She was beginning to think she'd have been better off with Amos. At least she knew what he wanted.

"Mr. MacGregor," she ventured, swallowing a dryness in her throat. "Are you . . . running from the police?"

"No!" He looked at her in surprise, and then smiled. "No." He went back to looking out the window. He seemed pensive, subdued. It occurred to her that he was deliberately making himself seem less vibrant, less alive. Less threatening. "I like it here, Delilah. I could use a place like this right now. Quiet, peaceful, no phone—"

"No phone!" She pounced with the air of one crying, "Ah-hah!" "I thought you wanted a phone."

"To call out," he said pointedly.

"Then you are trying to avoid somebody." She took a deep breath. "Mr. MacGregor, it seems to me that you are the one who needs a favor."

Seconds ticked slowly by. He wasn't a very good liar, she thought, noting the tension in his shoulders. She wondered if he would decide to tell her the truth, and whether she'd be able to tell . . .

Crossly, and with a touch of embarrassment, he said, "All right. When I . . . uh, landed in your field, I was on my way to see someone."

A woman, Delilah supplied silently. Of course.

Luke coughed and continued in a reluctant mutter. "She wants me to get married."

"Married?" He'd managed to surprise her. And was she just a tiny bit . . . disappointed?

He nodded solemnly. "Immediately, if not sooner. She's very determined."

"I don't believe it," Delilah murmured disgustedly.

Luke looked pained. "Believe it. You don't know how persistent Glenna can be when she gets obsessed with something."

Delilah gazed sourly at him. It wasn't his story she didn't believe—his voice had the unmistakable timbre of sincerity. She couldn't believe she'd been taken in by his charm and good looks. He was a cowardly, egocentric jerk. "Have you tried just telling her you don't want to get married?" she asked tartly.

"It's not that easy," he said with a put-upon sigh. "I care about Glenna—a lot. I don't want to hurt her, but we just don't see eye-to-eye on the subject of marriage. Since I'm not busy right now, she's expecting me to get serious about it. I don't want to have it out with her. I don't want to hurt her. But if I were to make myself inaccessible . . ." His eyes crinkled ruefully. "So . . . how about it? Satisfied that my motives are, if not honorable, at least valid?"

Delilah was silent. She didn't know why she should feel depressed. It was just what she should have expected of someone with his looks, charm, and magnetism. She felt very sorry for the poor woman whose misfortune it was to be in love with this man. She would be doing Glenna a very big favor by preventing her from marrying a man who didn't even have the guts to face up to her with the truth! How awful it must be to be so emotionally dependent on a man. It was a state Delilah vowed never to find herself in!

"I don't know," she muttered finally, biting her lip. "It seems . . . I'd have to think about it. There are problems."

"What problems?"

She ran a hand through her hair, uncaring that the gesture invariably made her look like a street urchin.

"Well, for starters, I don't know where I'd put you. I only have one room."

Luke shrugged, smiling. "I don't mind. I can sleep on the couch."

She eyed him and said stonily, "I was thinking in terms of the barn."

"Ouch." He winced, then grinned. "Delilah, are you afraid of me?"

"Afraid, no," she retorted scornfully. "Realistic, yes. And you aren't. Do you have any idea at all what you'd be getting into?"

"What do you mean?"

"Have you ever seen a birth before? *Any* birth?" When he shook his head blithely she eyed his beautiful jacket and snowy shirt and said flatly, "It's very messy."

He made a scout's-honor sign. "I promise to change my clothes first."

"Hmm," she murmured skeptically. "You know there's no such thing as nine to five on a farm."

"There's no such thing as nine to five when you own a company, either," he said quietly.

"I'd have to be able to depend on you. Really *depend* on you. A lamb's favorite time to be born is three o'clock in the morning. It's cold and dark, and you have to get out of bed and sit in the cold and *wait*. Sometimes we'll be up all night and work right through the next day—and the next night we might be up all night again—"

He took her arms and interrupted her with his quiet voice. "But if I'm here helping you it wouldn't be like that, would it? We'd take turns."

Delilah swallowed. "I don't want to lose a lamb because you decided to sleep through your turn to check the ewes. And if I need your help—"

"I'll be there. You can count on it." There was a soft, thoughtful look in his eyes. "Any other objections?"

Oh, yes, she thought, there were other objections. But she couldn't very well say, "You're too attractive. I don't know how to breathe when you're close to me." Just for a moment she allowed herself to imagine what it would be like to work alongside this man, to share the long night vigils, to have an extra pair of hands and a strong back to help when trouble came. And a shoulder to lean on, arms to hold her when she cried with exhaustion and frustration . . .

She licked her lips. It was insane. She knew what kind of man he was. It was crazy. And, of course, out of the question.

"I—I'll think about it," she finally said.

"Good." Luke was smiling at her, maddeningly confident, sure of himself, sure of her. "Well, while you're thinking it over, why don't we go find that phone, and I'll buy some clothes more suitable for delivering lambs—just in case."

He really was sure she was going to give in, she thought. And why shouldn't he be? He probably didn't hear an unequivocal "no" very often. And why in the world hadn't she been able to give him that firm answer herself? Indecision wasn't usually part of her makeup. She glanced out the window, biting at her lower lip. "It's late," she mumbled distractedly. "I don't know where the time goes. It's too near chore time. I can't go now. You'll have to wait. . . ."

"Listen, tell you what." Luke was positively overflowing with expansive good humor. "Why don't you let me go into town in your pickup? I can get some clothes, make my calls, and you can stay here and do your chores and make up your mind. I can even run any errands you might have, pick up some groceries. See how nice it can be, having an extra hand?"

Delilah hesitated a moment longer and then capitulated. Maybe without his disturbing presence she could think of a way to say "no" and make it stick. "Okay," she agreed at last. "Keys are in the pickup. Watch the brakes on the downhill grade."

"Gotcha." Halfway out the door he stopped and turned. "Do you have a grocery list?"

"Um . . . I don't really have time—"

"Never mind, I'll do without. See you later."

"I'll get you some money—I'll pay you *later*," she said to the closing door. A moment later she heard her pickup cough grumpily and go snarling away down the road.

All through her chores she kept imagining what it might be like to have the president of Thermodyne sleeping in her barn, hauling water and hay to her sheep. All she had to do was remember what had happened this morning when he'd tried to handle old number 907 to know that it could be highly entertaining. He was so . . . confident. So arrogant. The thought of a man who looked as if he could model for *Gentlemen's Quarterly*, up to his immaculate elbows in wet, slippery newborn lambs was incredibly appealing.

And interrupting her more coherent thoughts were other, more nebulous and far more disturbing images and impressions: just-washed hair with a life of its own; a strange good-morning kiss; a husky voice with erotic overtones, murmuring, "Come help me, love."

Like her temper, her fantasies had a tendency to get away from her now and then.

But Delilah was a practical person and, as she'd told Luke, a realist. Her house was small, but it suited her perfectly. It was a cozy house. *Intimate*. She might be able to get away with making Luke sleep in the barn, but he'd still be eating with her, sharing the bathroom, long spring evenings . . .

By the time she'd settled down to milk the goat it was dark, and she'd finally come to terms with the real reason she didn't want Luke staying on. It had come to her inescapably at dusk, when she'd heard her pickup grumbling up the road and had reacted with pounding heart and weak knees. She was intensely attracted to Luke MacGregor. The very fact that deep down inside she really wanted him to stay was the best reason she could think of for telling him to go. She couldn't have that kind of complication and distraction right now. As she'd told Roy Underwood, men just didn't fit in with her life's goals and ambitions, and that went double for a man like Luke MacGregor!

She'd tell him no. She would. Just as soon as she got to the house . . .

About ten yards from her door she stopped dead, the milk bucket in her hand. There was warmth and light pouring from the windows, and with it the most incredible, mouth-watering, stomach-twisting smell.

Lady came and sat down on her boots. Delilah dropped a hand to the dog's head and was rewarded with the white flash of a canine grin. "Hush," she murmured absently. "I can hear you drooling."

She swallowed hard, climbed the steps, and pushed open the door.

The president of Thermodyne, dressed in new khaki work clothes and wearing a floral-print flour-sack dish towel knotted around his hips, looked up and quickly doused his cigarette under a stream of water from the kitchen faucet. "Sorry," he said, looking guilty. "I keep forgetting. I always smoke while I'm cooking. Keeps me from eating."

Delilah stared blankly at him, then realized that she must have been standing there sniffing the wind like a hunting dog. "No, no," she murmured impatiently, then asked fearfully, "Is that . . . *steak* I smell cooking?"

"Yeah." Luke slid a loaf of foil-wrapped French bread onto the oven's lower rack and turned back to the sink, where he began assaulting a head of lettuce. "You just about have time to wash up—unless you like your steak well done, in which case you could probably manage a shower."

"Medium rare," Delilah said faintly. Sizzling and popping under the red glow of the broiler were two of the biggest T-bones she'd ever seen. With what he'd paid for them she could have eaten for a week. She caught the unmistakable glimmer of red among the chunks of crisp green in the salad bowl. She happened to know the off-season price of tomatoes at the local markets.

That was the clincher. He had to go. She couldn't afford him. She was pretty sure she didn't have enough money left in the house to repay him for the groceries.

But, she told herself as she washed her hands, there was no use crying over spilled milk. The damage was done, the food was here, and she couldn't send it back. The only thing to do was enjoy it.

"It was too late to get the potatoes in," Luke said airily, blissfully unaware of her consternation. "You know, with your lifestyle, what you need is a microwave oven. You can bake a potato in five minutes in a microwave."

"Wonderful," Delilah murmured as she lowered herself weakly into a chair. She wondered if the presence of potatoes meant he'd also bought sour cream. She coughed and stared fixedly at her hands. "How much do I owe you?"

He didn't answer except to set a plate before her almost reverently, like an offering. Delilah swallowed again, but kept her hands primly folded in her lap, reminding herself that she was a civilized person and must not, therefore, fall upon her plate like a ravenous wolf.

When the silence had become noticeable and Luke still hadn't taken his place at the table, she looked up to find him watching her, leaning on his hands, one of which was on the tabletop. The other was on the back of her chair. His eyes, shielded and unreadable, were very close to hers. "Don't worry about it," he said softly. "It's on me."

"Uh-uh. No." Pride alone propelled her upward. When she found herself nose to nose with a face handsome enough to melt mirrors, she sank back down, trying to blink into focus.

"It's the least I can do," Luke said, smiling with devastating effect. "I'd have taken you out to dinner, but I didn't think you'd want to leave your sheep, so I did the next best thing. I brought dinner to you." He dropped a kiss neatly on the end of her nose and moved away from her to pick up his own plate. "Besides, I like to eat, and I don't mean peanut butter and oatmeal. If I'm going to work for you, I'm going to need real food." He glanced up at her, noticed that she hadn't yet tackled her steak, and made an impatient gesture with his knife. "Come on, eat. That's an order."

"Are you as good at taking orders?" Delilah asked

dryly, finally allowing herself to pick up her knife and fork. Luke lifted his eyebrows interrogatively, and she added, "You don't get to be the president of a corporation because you like taking orders. How do you think you'd like taking orders from me?"

He frowned thoughtfully, then said with a slow, lazy smile, "Well, it would probably depend a lot on what the order was, but on a temporary basis I think I could handle it. Does this mean you've made up your mind to hire me?"

"No," Delilah said, frowning. "It doesn't."

"Take your time." His smile was positively beatific. Still so confident . . . so sure. How she longed to turn him down once and for all, to wipe that smug look off his face. If he thought he could buy her with a few groceries, even if some of those groceries were steak and sour cream . . .

Why not? she thought almost defiantly. Why shouldn't she let him stay? What harm could it do? She was a grown woman, and she seriously doubted he was a rapist or an ax murderer, and, what was more important, he wasn't after her land!

And deep down inside, and maybe not so deep at that, was the fear that, in spite of her bravado, she really couldn't handle ninety-five lambing ewes single-handedly. What if she got sick? What if, faced with the probability of disaster, she was forced to turn to Amos? There might be something very fishy about Luke MacGregor, but he was infinitely preferable to Amos.

And if that was so, why did the man make her feel so threatened?

Luke interrupted her silent debate by lobbing a dish towel into her lap. "Okay, you dry, I'll wash. It would be fairer if you did all the clean-up, since I did the cooking, but I'll overlook it just this once. We can work out the details later—if you let me stay." He put his hands on the back of her chair and leaned over to whisper in her ear, "*Are* you?"

"What?" she asked vaguely.

"Going to let me stay?"

He wasn't touching her, not really. And yet she could *feel* him there—his breath on the side of her face, on her neck, his hands on the back of the chair, his body on the other side of it. She could feel the heat of his body as if it, and not the hard, unyielding wood of the chair, supported her back and thighs.

As if propelled by a spring, Delilah lurched out of the chair. Luke watched her quizzically as she walked to a drawer beside the stove and took out a flashlight.

"What's that for?"

She hesitated, slapping the flashlight against her palm, then drew a deep, steadying breath. "I'm going to make you a bed in the barn." Frowning at the middle button on Luke's shirt, she added, "It's too late to go into town tonight. I'll . . . um . . . "

His hand touched the flashlight and then closed on her wrist. Very softly, lightly chafing her wrist with his thumb, he said, "I didn't think you were serious about the barn."

She looked at him intrepidly, but couldn't answer. The fingers on her wrist were generating queer little electrical impulses, and all she could think about was whether he would let go, and if he did, whether she would be sorry or glad.

"Why are you afraid to have me sleep in the same house with you? You weren't afraid last night."

"Last night," she said pointedly, "you were out cold."

He laughed softly, and his eyes held hers. "You don't trust me?"

With a lift of her chin Delilah countered, "Should I?"

His lips relaxed and curved into a smile of captivating sweetness. "Absolutely." Delilah realized that her chest was hurting, and released a long-held breath. "Delilah, I'd never do anything you didn't want me to do. . . . "

It was his voice, she decided, that was mesmerizing her. Or perhaps it was some uncataloged narcotic that radiated from him like body heat.

"All you have to do," he murmured, "is say . . . *no.*" But when his head descended, that word was the farthest thing from her mind. The warm satin of his lips became the moist heat of his mouth. Her eyelids fluttered and drifted down as she unconsciously tilted her head, opening her mouth to the gentle thrust of his tongue.

His breath whispered through her mouth in a little sigh. His hands moved, pulling her to his body by slow, inexorable degrees, so that her breasts first just barely brushed, then were flattened against his chest, and his thighs touched hers, then lined up hard against them. His hand pressed on her waist, bringing the soft inward curve of her belly against the contours of his lower body.

Something hit her hard in the chest. Her heart began a slow thundering that sent waves of heat through her body with every pulse, while her breath rushed upward, like effervescence seeking release. It made a low, whimpering sound as it escaped her mouth, only to be captured in his. Her hands had somehow found their way to the back of his neck. She could feel the thick softness of his hair beneath her fingers. . . .

She jerked her hands down and pushed furiously against his chest. Luke resisted the pressure effortlessly, releasing her slowly, and in his own sweet time. "I still haven't heard you say it . . . no."

Delilah pressed the back of her hand to her lips, hiding them from that dark gaze, knowing they were moist and swollen from his kiss. She glared at him as she struggled to corral her breathing and her poise, then gave up and turned on her heel. Stalking into her bedroom, she snatched up one of her two pillows, her handmade patchwork comforter, and the extra blanket she kept folded at the foot of her bed, and returned to push the whole untidy load into Luke's arms.

"You'll find a bale of straw in the first stall to the left," she said through the tension in her jaws. "Wire cutters are on the second shelf. Use as much of it as you need."

"Delilah—"

She opened the door and stood implacably, letting in cold air. Her voice trembled—with the chill, she told herself: "I guess you must have heard what Amos called me. But I'm not. I assure you, I'm not what he said I was."

Luke's voice was very quiet. "I never thought you were."

"Then why did you think I'd—"

"I gave you every opportunity to stop me. You didn't."

"This isn't going to work." She was beginning to shiver, both with cold and delayed reaction to an embrace that had upset her in ways she would never, ever want to admit. "Please . . . tomorrow I'll take you to town. Now, if you don't mind, I think I'd like to go to bed."

"At eight o'clock?"

"I've been up since six!"

" 'Lilah," he whispered slowly, "you've really got a problem, haven't you?"

"Yes." She sighed. "But by tomorrow he'll be gone. Please, Mr. MacGregor . . ."

He hesitated a moment longer, then muttered, " 'Night, 'Lilah," and went down the steps. A few yards from the house she saw him switch on the flashlight, and she quietly closed the door.

Her house had always seemed so warm and secure, yet after Luke had gone, it seemed untidy and uncomfortable. Delilah felt keyed up and restless, exposed and vaguely frightened, as though something unknown and dangerous was prowling the shadows beyond the firelight. She felt as though Luke were watching her, even while she undressed, took a shower, washed her lingerie. And she was haunted by the same sensual images that had tormented her all afternoon, augmented now by more recent experiences. His thumb, slowly stroking the cords of her wrist; the hard muscles of his thighs pressing against hers; the unexpected feel of the back of his neck in her hands, so vibrantly, shockingly *intimate*.

That was what bothered her about the man—he'd never been a stranger. From the moment she'd leaned her body into his and taken his weight across her shoulders, there had been a sense of familiarity, of rightness. And yet she found him frightening, disturbing. It should have been a contradiction, but it wasn't. Delilah new that Luke MacGregor was frightening and disturbing mainly because she was fighting so hard against that familiarity. What would happen if she were to stop fighting it . . . accept it . . . give in to it? Could he touch her mind and heart as he'd already touched her body, make her want to lose herself in him as she was longing to surrender to the warmth of his body?

She angrily piled her clean lingerie into a pan to hang out in the morning, turned out the lights, and walked to the window to stand staring up at the barn. Her mouth still tingled with the imprint of his, and her breasts ached and swelled in involuntary reaction to the memory of their contact with his chest. All right, she admitted, she'd never felt like this before, but she'd been fooled before too. Every time she had been left with the bitter aftertaste of disappointment. Her few sexual experiences had left her feeling lonely and betrayed. Why should this man, a man who would stoop so low as to hide from a woman who loved him, be any different? In the one short day he'd been in her life he'd turned it upside down and torn to shreds what little peace of mind she had.

No. She'd take him to town first thing in the morning, right after chores. He could go back where he belonged, and she would get back to what was important—to her sheep, her future, her dream.

Up in the darkness near the barn door a tiny light flared. The glow of the match briefly illuminated cupped hands, a classic profile. It seemed the president of Thermodyne was restless too.

Luke drew smoke deeply and gratefully into his lungs—and erupted into a fit of coughing. Examining the end of the cigarette as if it were responsible for all his troubles, he heaved a long, discouraged sigh. Delilah was right, he thought. He could be skiing right now—or more probably be snuggled up to a warm fire, a warm drink, and a warm body, in no particular order and probably simultaneously.

She was an even bigger pain than her father. Why wa
he putting up with this aggravation, anyway? He ough
to say the heck with it—cut his losses, pull up stakes
and go to Idaho, Montana . . . even Alaska. He'd alway
wanted to go to Alaska. . . .

She'd surprised him, he mused. He kept rememberin
the way she'd felt in his arms. She'd come to him so eas
ily, so naturally. And yet . . .

Somehow it had gone wrong. For perhaps the firs
time in his life, he'd misplayed his hand. He couldn'
read her, that was the problem. She had a thick hid
and was as headstrong as a billy goat, but he could sti
feel her fingers stroking the hair back from his fore
head—right after she'd stitched his head together as i
she were sewing a button on a shirt! And just now . .
her mouth, warm and sweet, and her hands on the bacl
of his neck . . .

Dammit, he needed more *time*. Time to figure her out
time to get in under all those defenses she'd built u
around herself. And she was bound and determined t
ship him off tomorrow morning, just as soon as sh
could drive him into town!

Drive him . . . When the inspiration struck him, it fel
like a discreet tap on the shoulder by a helpful guardia
angel. Or devil. A very small voice said, If she can't driv
you, she can't get rid of you.

He straightened abruptly, tossing his cigarette awa
in a shower of sparks. The house was dark. Off to th
side, all by itself under the silver glow of starlight, sa
the Incredible Hulk, as he'd begun to call it on the wa
home from town—Delilah's twenty-year-old Navy
surplus pickup. Grinning to himself, Luke sat down i
the barn doorway and took off his shoes, and then
tucking the flashlight under his arm, set off across th
gentle slope of bare ground that separated the barn from
the house. Lady came running up to lick his hand, ther
went ranging off on some foray of her own.

He felt for the truck's hood latch, praying that i
wouldn't open with a creak and a groan, but his guard
ian angel was still on the job. The latch gave, and the

hood rose with only the faintest metallic whisper. And then Lucas Byron Charles MacGregor, president and principal stockholder of Thermodyne, Inc., and erstwhile law-abiding citizen, working only with the aid of starlight, flashlight, and a watchful guardian angel, calmly and deftly removed the rotor from the distributor of Delilah Beaumont's pickup.

Five

The smell of bacon cooking woke Delilah out of a heavy sleep. She lay for a moment with her eyes closed, floating in a dream limbo that must have had its origins in the furthest reaches of her subconscious memory, before the years of housekeepers and cold breakfasts, when loving hands had tied ribbons in her hair and a soft voice had sung her to sleep with nursery rhymes. . . .

She blinked her eyes open and stretched, then saw the rectangle of pale light on the Navaho rug that covered her feet, and remembered: *Luke.* And to make things worse, she had overslept. Kicking herself free of the rug, she scrambled out of bed and snatched up the alarm clock, glaring at it in silent reproach.

From the other room came the unmistakable clatter of stainless steel. Delilah hastily replaced the offending clock on the nightstand, fluffed her hair vigorously with her fingers, and dressed. She stripped off the warm thermals circumstances had forced her to sleep in, then quickly slipped on fresh underwear. The thermals went back on, then clean jeans and a sweat shirt. Half-hopping on one foot, still struggling with her tennis shoe, she went out into the warm living room.

" 'Morning, sunshine."

Luke had turned to zap her with one of his high-voltage smiles. It caught her mid-hop, and she had to drop down onto the couch and pretend to be absorbed in tying her shoes to give herself time to recover.

Damn, she thought. How could any mortal man look so good so early in the day? And she'd always considered herself a morning person! He'd already helped himself to her shower, obviously, and his damp hair still had a tousled, Huck Finn look. There was nothing boyish, however, about the arrangement of muscles in his neck and shoulders. How could a man look so masculine wearing a dish towel for an apron?

And this room, already warm, full of golden light and mouth-watering smells . . . It was just too much. Getting out of a warm bed in a cold, dark house had never been her favorite part of the day. This was so wonderful, and yet, perversely, she resented it. She felt usurped, her confidence in her independence severely shaken.

When she finally got up off the couch, Luke met her with a cup of coffee. "What'd you do, just walk in?" she asked irritably, without returning his greeting.

"I knocked," he said equably, "but you were sleeping. Seemed like a good time to take a shower. How do you like your eggs?"

Delilah stared at him for a moment, then murmured, "Over easy." She strolled in an offhand way to the stove, lifted the paper towel that coverd a plateful of bacon, and selected one perfect, crisp red-brown slice. She leaned against the counter and nibbled, then blissfully closed her eyes.

"Do you *like* to cook?" she asked after a moment, licking her fingers and watching Luke sprinkle salt and pepper over slowly congealing eggs. Lacy yellow bubbles had begun to pop and sizzle around the edges of the whites. Delilah wondered if it was real butter.

Luke glanced over at her, his expression wry. "Not especially. I like to *eat,* and if I can't get someone else to do it for me . . ." He shrugged and turned his attention back to the eggs. "Ooops. Damn. How do you feel about broken yolks?"

"That one's yours," Delilah helped herself to another piece of bacon. "Don't you have a housekeeper?" she asked, then thought, Or does the girl who wants to marry you take care of that too?

"When I have a house." He flashed her another crooked smile. "Most of the time I live on drilling sites—trailers, R.V.'s, maybe an apartment, if there's a place close enough."

"Like Mammoth?"

He shrugged, busy dishing up eggs. "I have a place in Mammoth, but I spend most of my time on-site." He turned with a plate in each hand and nodded toward the table. "Shall we?"

She took her plate and sat down, a little awed by the fact that, though she'd already eaten two strips of bacon, there were four more on her plate. Luke put two pieces of bread in the toaster and gracefully straddled the chair opposite her.

He was wearing his khakis again. The shirt was short-sleeved and open at the neck. Delilah stared at the pattern of hair on his tanned forearms and decided she knew exactly what Luke MacGregor was up to. He thought he could get to her through her stomach. . . .

And he was succeeding. She felt mellow and relaxed, and there was a nice core of warmth in her middle that had already begun to radiate to other parts of her. Last night seemed long ago and unimportant. She'd been neurotic and unreasonable; the kiss had merely been friendly. And if he slept in the barn . . .

"I'm sorry," she said, giving her head a shake, "what did you say?"

"I said, 'What time shall I be ready to leave?' "

"Oh." Delilah coughed and reached for her coffee, frowning and feigning deep thought. She was trying to think of a way of withdrawing her edict while saving her pride. "Let me see. I'm getting a late start. . . ." He was gazing at her with a patently innocent look that told her he knew very well he had her wavering. "It usually takes me about an hour and a half—what time is it now?—and then I'll have to—" She stopped. She'd been staring over Luke's shoulder, thinking out loud, and it had just registered that something that should have been in her line of vision wasn't there.

"Where," she said in a frozen voice, "is the pan I left next to the sink?"

"Pan?"

"Pan. The one with—"

"Oh, you mean the pan of underwear? I hung them—"

But Delilah was already out the door. On the top step she teetered to a halt. Yes, sir, there they were, every last article of them, stirring gently, almost voluptuously, in the brilliant morning air—camisoles and teddies, lacy bras and wispy bikini panties, in champagne and rose petal, honeyed peach and baby blue, naughty black and purest white. Her secret vice and only vanity . . .

She'd always loved pretty, lacy things. As a motherless child raised by a stern father and no-nonsense house-keepers, though, she'd been dressed "sensibly," with an eye to practicality and minimum upkeep. Her hair had been low-maintenance short. Her clothes, including her underwear, had been serviceable, machine-washable, no-iron cotton blends. It had never occurred to Delilah to *ask* for what she wanted—she was much too proud for that—and so she had secretly coveted the ruffles and frills her friends wore to one another's birthday parties, and had taken to daydreaming over mail-order catalogs. When she was in high school she saved enough money and sent off an order, the first of many. Long after she'd accepted the fact that she was never going to be the ruffles-and-lace type, she'd continued to take a secret measure of reassurance and confidence from the knowledge that underneath her defensive, tomboy exterior, under her jeans and funky T-shirts. she really was a *girl.*

It was a side of herself she guarded jealously. Of her current circle of acquaintants, only Mara Jane knew. And now there was Luke, the last person in the world she'd have wanted to possess such a potent weapon. She felt stripped and violated, more vulnerable than she'd ever felt before in her life.

Luke had come to stand in the doorway, hands on his

hips, head tilted quizzically. Delilah turned slowly, hugging her burgeoning anger close, trying desperately to keep him from seeing how important it was to her.

"What gave you the right to do this?" she asked.

He lifted his hand to his scalp, looking incredulous and utterly bewildered. "The right? I was trying to help."

"Yeah, well, do me a favor—don't help me," Delilah said tightly, moving to brush past him. His hand gripped the doorframe, making a barricade of his arm. She stared at him, tight-lipped and tense with unreasoning resentment.

" 'Lilah," he said softly, "I have a sister."

"I'm not your sister!" she shot back.

"I know."

There they were again, she thought, those crazy dissonances that seemed to rasp across every nerve in her body, raising bumps and shivers that cried out to be stroked and soothed, held and comforted. Just two words—*I know*—and his eyes, dark and unreadable, dropping, as if compelled, to the front of her sweat shirt. He did know. He was Superman, he had X-ray vision. He could see right through her baggy clothes to her satin chemise, and beyond that to her skin, no doubt flushing a deep dusty rose with mortification. And every time he looked at her from now on he would know. . . .

The silent interval lenghtened. Delilah didn't know whether she felt more like shouting at him or bursting into tears. After a long moment Luke shook his head and let his arm drop, and she slipped past him.

"I'll be through with the chores in an hour," she said jerkily as she snatched up her windbreaker and gloves. "Please be ready to leave."

When she lurched back out the door she found Luke where she had left him, lounging against the frame, thumbs hooked in his hip pockets. She doubted that he'd even heard her last statement. As he basked in the early-morning sunshine his eyes were focused on the clothesline, and his lips were curved in a smile of rapt fascination. Her underthings, it seemed, didn't share her reservations. Stirred by the ever-present breezes, they flirted outrageously, undulating coyly and with an unbridled sensuousness they certainly never enjoyed when she was wearing them!

Delilah put her head down and stomped up to the barn, blotting out the sight by visualizing hideous medieval tortures featuring the handsome president of Thermodyne, Inc.

"I can't understand it," Delilah said for the fourth time. "It's never done this before. I've never had a bit of trouble with it."

The pickup's starter growled ineffectually a few more times, gave a dispirited "clunk," and lapsed into silence.

"Maybe it's flooded," Luke offered helpfully.

She firmly shook her head and reached for the door handle. "It's never flooded before. I'm going to take a look."

"Stay there. I'll look while you try to turn it over."

"Do you know anything about engines?"

"I'm an engineer," he said loftily, climbing out of the cab. A moment later his voice came from under the hood. "Try it now." And then, "Okay—*now*." And still later, "How's this?" He came walking back to the cab, dusting his hands and shaking his head. "Might be your starter." He sounded dubious.

Delilah hoped her expression told him what she thought of his mechanical aptitude. "It's probably flooded," she muttered as she reluctantly abandoned the fight and climbed out of the truck, giving it a look of reproach as she slammed the door. "The way my life's been going lately, it figures."

"You can try it after a while," Luke said soothingly. "After you've—*it's* cooled down."

She threw him another blistering glare and stalked up the hill toward the pasture. It wasn't fair, she thought. She'd been invaded by an alien. First her pasture, then her house, her bed, her kitchen, and now the most personal, private place of all—her fantasies. What next? Was there no sanctuary from this man?

"So," Luke asked cheerfully, striding buoyantly along beside her, "what's on your schedule for today?"

"Why?" she asked shortly.

"Oh, I don't know. I thought I might as well give you a hand. I've got nothing better to do while I'm waiting. And," he added, holding his arms out wide just in case she might not have noticed his brawny arms and khaki-clad chest, "I'm even dressed for it."

Delilah postponed her answer by climbing deftly and unhesitatingly over the pasture fence. After one doubtful look at the strand of barbed wire along the top of the fence, Luke followed. Delilah heard his muffled oath and grinned, her spirits beginning to rise a little. She paused to allow Luke, muttering profanely and rubbing his thigh, to catch up.

"I still have to sort those ewes," she told him, plowing steadily across the corner of the pasture toward the holding pen, purposely choosing a shortcut that would take them over yet another fence. She gave him a considering look. "I guess you could be of some help at that."

He folded his arms on his chest, an unconsciously macho stance, full of self-confidence. "Just tell me what you want me to do."

She pursed her lips to hide a smile and nodded. The day was definitely improving as it went along. "Okay," she said agreeably. "All the ewes will lamb over a period of about three weeks. It's hard to keep a close watch on so many, so to cut the odds, I divide them into groups—first week, second week—"

"Okay, I got that." He gave her a sideways glance. "You . . . don't figure this out by the sort of hands-on examination I witnessed yesterday?"

She shook her head. "No, that's for the final sorting. I go by the numbers. Breeding records." She took a folded piece of notebook paper from the pocket of her windbreaker and held it out to him. "Those are the numbers of the ones I'll separate out today. They should all lamb during the first week."

"Numbers?" Luke was scanning the list. "What's this 'red 104'? 'Purple 911'?"

"Ear tags." She climbed the fence, and paused with one leg over the top to look down at him. "Coming?" she challenged.

He gave a pained sigh and followed, but took more time and care. When he landed lightly in the dusty pen, several ewes lying in the immediate vicinity chewing their cud lurched to their feet and stood stamping at the intruder in their midst.

"You can man the gate." Delilah told him as she moved off through the milling flock. She could feel him following, moving gingerly.

"Can you be more specific?" he asked.

She explained with exaggerated patience that he was to hold the gate to the pasture, opening it to let out unwanted animals, and closing it to thwart the escape of the ones she chose to keep.

"Think you can handle that?" she asked. She knew she was deliberately taunting him, but in fact the job wasn't as easy as it sounded. She was beginning to look forward to the morning's work.

"I think so," Luke said dryly, refusing to be goaded. He handed her the list.

"You keep it. I'll call out the ear-tag numbers to you, and you can tell me whether they're on the list or not."

"Okay, sure."

"Ready?"

He lifted his shoulders and grinned. Delilah grinned back. "Okay, city boy—let's see how it goes."

It went well. Surprisingly and disappointingly well. Luke had good reflexes and enough strength to wield the heavy wooden gate with a degree of precision that Delilah couldn't have managed. Time after time she would shout, "Let that one go!" and watch the gate swing open at just the right moment, only to slam back in the nick of time to frustrate the head-down escape run of the animal right behind. By midmorning she was covered with dust and sweat and was thoroughly out of sorts, and Luke was lounging against the gatepost looking as gorgeous as ever and handling his job with his usual grace, and even with a certain flair. Delilah kept throwing him glances, more of frustration than of grudging admiration. His comeuppance was not proceeding as planned.

Just before noon, with only a few animals yet to be culled from the flock in the holding pen, Delilah paused, frowning, to wipe sweat from her forehead with her shirtsleeve.

"What about 907, Luke? Is she on that list?"

"Yeah . . . with a question mark."

"Right. I remember now. I don't have a date on her, but when I checked her yesterday I thought she seemed to be showing some development. I'm going to check her again, just to be sure."

But the canny Suffolk had learned something from the previous day's experience. Once Delilah had a grip on her, she displayed a degree of intelligence rare in sheep, and directed her charge straight into the heart of the milling flock. A short, placid Hampshire set a perfect screen, and Delilah, trying to maintain her grip on one animal's neck while leaping over the other, tripped and fell face down in dust and well-trampled sheep manure.

Sheep are very sure-footed. Delilah wasn't trampled, and nothing was hurt except her dignity. Before she could even shake herself, she felt hands on her waist, back, shoulders, hair; heard Luke's voice, taut with alarm.

" 'Lilah! 'Lilah, are you all right? Come on, Blue Eyes, say something."

He rolled her over and, to her absolute astonishment and dismay, picked her up out of the dirt and cradled her in his arms like a helpless child.

"Dammit, Luke!" she hollered. "Get the gate!" She struggled briefly, but it was already too late. Number 907 had bulldozed her way through the untended gate and was bounding across the pasture like an obese antelope. Delilah folded her arms and glared up into Luke's face. "Well, I hope you're satisfied."

Luke looked slightly dazed. His eyes followed the escapee, then came back to hers, dark and unreadable. "Look—" His voice was rusty. "I thought you were hurt."

"Well, I'm not. So put me down. Please."

He hesitated for what seemed to Delilah an inordinate amount of time, then set her feet on the ground. She lurched awkwardly and had to clutch at him for balance. His hands closed on her arms, just above the elbows.

" 'Lilah, I'm sorry about the ewe," he said softly. "What can I do to help?"

She almost said, "What ewe?" She wondered if she'd been trampled after all. It sure *felt* as if an unruly ewe had run roughshod over her chest. Luke was too close. He always seemed to be too close. She felt crowded, half-suffocated. She licked her lips and tasted dust. If he just weren't so good-looking, she thought. If only he weren't always so . . . *together*, so in command. He made her feel surly and childish, grubby and—

Oh, Lord, she thought, what must she look like?

"It's no big deal," she mumbled, addressing the middle of his chest. "I'll get her tonight or tomorrow when I feed them." She wiped a hand across her face in a futile attempt to remove some of the mask of dirt. She was angry with him for standing there smiling at her with his lethal eyes, angry with herself for caring what she looked like. Angry because for the first time her life seemed to be out of her control. Dammit, her life was planned! She guided her own destiny. She *did* things— things did not *happen* to her! But all of a sudden it seemed as though life had its head down, and all she could do was hang on.

Luke chuckled softly, intimately, and began to wipe her face with his hands. After a moment he said, "I'm afraid it's beyond me. Aren't we about finished here?"

Delilah was absolutely incapable of speech, but managed to nod.

"Tell you what," he murmured, still holding her face in his hands, "why don't you go clean up while I fix us some lunch?" Before she could respond, he kissed her, dirt and all. "Hmm," he said consideringly, licking his lips, then he laughed and tucked her hand in the crook of his arm.

Delilah yanked it angrily away, but after a moment

she followed him out of the pen and down the hill, like a lamb trotting meekly at its mother's heels.

"You know what you need?" Luke said, chewing thoughtfully and gazing at some indeterminate spot in the middle of the orchard. "A runway. Some kind of . . . loading chute connecting this door with your holding pen."

Delilah snorted ambiguously. She was still smarting from the morning's humiliating turnabout, but his perceptiveness surprised her. A runway was exactly what she needed. She hoped to build one with some of the money from this year's lamb crop.

"Thanks," she said dryly. "I never would have thought of that."

He threw her an unrepentant grin. "I can't help it—I'm a problem solver. Show me a problem and I try to figure out a solution. It's a reflex."

"A problem solver—is what you call yourself? I'd call you a *buttinski.*"

She was sitting on an overturned barrel beside the barn's back door. During lambing she would use the barrel for water, but now, warmed by the sun, it made a good spot for a picnic lunch. The lunch consisted of sandwiches—sweet-smoked and baked deli ham on pungent rye, with mustard and mayonnaise, crisp, fresh dill pickles, and thick slices of tomato—as sumptuous a feast as could be served up between two slices of bread. Luke was a few feet away, lounging against the barn's cement-block wall, looking completely at ease and unexpectedly natural in the rustic setting.

"Leave my problems alone," Delilah drawled lazily, listening to the mellow murmur of her own voice with mild surprise. She assured herself that it wasn't Luke's nearness that was taking the sting out of her remarks. It was only the sunshine. And the sandwich.

His response was equally lazy. "Now, that doesn't make sense, 'Lilah. What kind of person doesn't want her problems solved?"

"An independent person, maybe? I solve my own problems."

"Uh-uh. A bullheaded person. You'd just rather put up with a problem than have to admit you need help."

"Ha!" she said, gamely trying to give it her usual bite. "If I have a problem I'll ask for help." She pulled her feet up under her, so that she was perched cross-legged on the rounded side of the barrel—a precarious position at best. "I just don't see any need to get excited about a few inconveniences, especially when there's nothing I can do about it anyway. Accepting things you can't change—that's called *adapting*, Luke."

"I think I'd call it compromising," he rejoined mildly. "I don't care for it, myself."

She snorted. "It's called *surviving*. Things that can't learn to adapt to reality become extinct—like dodo birds and dinosaurs."

Luke shrugged. "Yes, but without the movers and shakers, the ones who wouldn't accept compromise, we'd all still be swinging from trees. There'd be no civilization."

"Humph," Delilah muttered, then added reluctantly, "Okay, it takes both kinds. But I am who I am. I've got to handle my problems *my* way." She wadded up the paper towel that had been serving as both plate and napkin and lofted it toward the brown paper bag at Luke's feet. She missed, and he stooped with characteristic grace to retrieve it.

"Okay, Popeye," he said, dropping the paper into the bag. "And *I* am who *I* am. And we've established that it takes both kinds to make things civilized." He strolled toward her and planted one booted foot firmly beside her on the barrel. "What do you think we could do about civilizing this place . . . working together?"

His voice was a purr full of all sorts of suggestions and subharmonies. Delilah hesitated, wondering what had happened to the air supply around her. And then, whether by accident or design, Luke's foot rocked the barrel backward.

Delilah uttered a strangled whoop and reached wildly

for the only thing that could prevent her from toppling over backward—Luke. As her hands gripped the unexpectedly solid bulk of his shoulders she felt herself caught and once again supported by a pair of strong, warm masculine arms. And even though she knew it was ridiculous, once again she really felt as though she'd forgotten how to breathe.

"How about it?" he murmured from an inch or so away. "Think we could build you a runway?"

"Mm," Delilah said.

"Tell me, how do you manage to get those animals from the holding pen, through the orchard, and into the barn?"

"It's a lot like stuffing feathers through the wrong end of a funnel," she whispered.

What an incredibly intimate thing laughter could be, she mused, when felt through another person's body rather than heard. Luke's laughter set up a corresponding vibration in her own stomach that made her want to break into giggles of pure joy. Fighting to hold on to a modicum of sanity, she cleared her throat and added, "But that's not the point. I don't have the materials to build a runway."

His eyes crinkled at her. "Sure, you do. There are posts and planks in that scrap pile over by the rams, and you have the roll of wire fencing you were using to divide the holding pen."

Delilah shook her head. "It's not enough. I've measured."

"Trust me," he said huskily. "I'm an engineer."

"But—"

"Come on. . . ." His words were silk on her eardrums, moist warmth on her cheek. "If I can design you a runway, will you help me build it?"

There was something wrong with the proposition, and she knew it. She just couldn't think, right this minute, what it was. She felt herself nodding. "Yes."

"Atta girl." Luke's laughter held a trace of smugness as he straightened, lowering Delilah gently to her feet. Squaring his shoulders and rubbing his hands together with thinly disguised self-congratulation, he announced, "Now, then, I'll need a few things."

"Lumber, for starters," she said dryly. Now that she could think again she was thinking, You big, arrogant know-it-all! She had remembered what it was about the "deal" she'd just struck with Luke that wasn't going to work. She'd figured and calculated it a thousand ways and knew, as well as she knew that there was an orange airplane in her pasture, that she didn't have enough material to build a runway.

"Hammer," Luke said, ignoring her comment. "Nails, baling wire, post-hole digger—"

"Will a shovel do?" she asked sweetly.

"I'll make it do. See, I can compromise." He gave her a dazzling smile and strode off, tossing over his shoulder as he ducked under the branch of an apple tree, "Oh—and see if you can find me a pair of gloves, while you're at it."

"And when did you get to be the boss here?" Delilah asked incredulously, but he was already out of earshot, purposefully sorting through a pile of planks.

Her temper was soaring, but then it occurred to her that if she gave him enough rope, Luke MacGregor might contrive his own comeuppance, much more effectively than anything she might dream up. And so she saluted smartly, smiled, and went off to find the articles he'd requested.

It promised to be a very entertaining afternoon.

Six

Luke was in a good mood. Both his projects—the wooing of Delilah Beaumont and the building of her sheep-run—were proceeding better than even he could have hoped. Not only was the run nearly finished, with time to spare before chores, but Delilah had been bubbling away beside him all afternoon in an unusually prolonged state of high spirits. It had been a surprise to discover that when she chose to be, Judge Beaumont's black-sheep daughter could be a real delight.

Building the run had been even easier than he'd expected. He couldn't understand why Delilah had put up such a fuss about it. A matter of pride, he supposed. Some people just couldn't stand to lose an argument. Digging the postholes had been the hardest part, and in spite of the gloves he had a couple of painful blisters to show for his afternoon's work. But other than that, it had just been a case of stretching the wire fencing along one side of the run and anchoring it to the posts with staples, then nailing the one-by-six planks into place along the other side. And Delilah had been proven wrong about those planks. As he'd calculated, there were more than enough of them to run two rows. The lowest was set at about eighteen inches—belly-high on those long-legged Suffolks. The highest was about head-high, leaving a gap of no more than a foot between. Of course, it was possible Delilah considered that the sides needed to be higher. He had an idea sheep might be good jumpers. But as narrow as the runway was, in order to prevent the sheep from turning around, he didn't see how they could get enough of a running start to jump the fence.

All in all, Luke was as proud of those two rickety-looking parallel fences as he was of anything he'd ever built. He felt like a kid putting together an electric train track. He could hardly wait to try it out.

A muffled "Damn!" came from the direction of the scrap-lumber pile. Luke paused with his mouth full of nails to aim a look of resigned annoyance at Delilah. For Pete's sake, he thought, why couldn't she follow the simplest, most logical suggestion? He'd already told her a dozen times to quit trying to sort through those heavy, splintery planks by herself. Why did she always have to be so damned independent? As far as he was concerned, if she'd hurt herself it served her right for being so bull-headed.

And it was obvious she'd hurt herself. She was standing with her head down, one hand clutched in the other, her slender shoulders hunched. She looked so small . . . like somebody's kid sister. When he saw her lean forward suddenly and tuck both hands between her legs, he put down his hammer and nails with a resigned sigh and went over to her.

"Here. Come on, 'Lilah, let me see."

She had to resist him, of course, as if he'd made an indecent suggestion. "It's nothing."

"Let me see it."

She lifted her eyes then—deep-set, black-fringed, sky-blue eyes, glazed with pain but still defiant. . . .

Once, while white-water rafting on the Colorado, Luke had had a steering oar get away from him and hit him squarely in the middle of his chest. There had been a few moments when he'd thought his heart had stopped beating. He was experiencing that same sensation now. He had a sudden and wholly unexpected urge to wrap his arms around Delilah and pull her against him, to hold her and stroke her hair and whisper idiotic nonsense words of comfort.

Her lips were having a disturbing and uncharacteristic tendency to tremble. It was all Luke could do to tear his gaze from them and look at the hand she was pulling unwillingly from its hiding place between her thighs. Much more roughly than he meant to, he ordered, "Come on. Quit stalling."

With a belligerent flip of her head she thrust her hand at him. "Look, it's no big deal. I jammed my finger a little, that's all. It's practically numb now anyway."

Luke peered closely at the index finger of her right hand and swallowed. "Jammed, hell," he said stonily. "You have a splinter. A big one. It's gone in under the nail, looks like halfway to the base." He caught her hand when she would have snatched it back. "Oh, no, you don't, Blue Eyes. That has to come out of there."

Stiff with hostility, she glared at him over their clasped hands. At last, unable to come up with anything better, she stuck her chin out and said with childish defiance, "Sez who?"

That unfamiliar wave of tenderness swept him again, and he fought to keep his face straight. "Sez me. Come on, you know you can't leave it like that."

She was breathing hard, like someone who was about to lose her temper, or start to cry. In her case he'd have bet it was temper. He couldn't imagine anything in the world that would make this woman cry. And he'd never met anyone, man or woman, who hated more the prospect of giving in.

"If you leave it in there," he said pleasantly and without emphasis, "it will fester and your fingernail will turn black and fall off and you'll get blood poisoning and die a slow and extremely agonizing death."

She whispered something uncomplimentary about Luke's antecedents. He raised his eyebrows and "tsk'd" reprovingly. "Well, I guess you can dish it out . . . but you can't take it," he drawled sadly.

"What's that supposed to mean?"

He tapped his head, and she responded with a snort. "Oh, sure," she said. "You were unconscious, remember? You *fainted.*"

"Feel free to faint if you want to. It's all right with me. Where can I find a needle and some tweezers?"

"Now I'm expected to hand my persecutor the thumb-screws?" She sighed. "I think there's a needle with my vet supplies in the barn. I don't have any tweezers. And I *never* faint. I'll probably just throw up. On *you*, with any luck at all . . ."

Delilah was saying, "Well, I guess you can take it, but you can't dish it out."

Her voice was so unusually soft and husky that Luke opened one eye and squinted at her from under his arm. She was sitting cross-legged in the straw near his feet, dousing her injured finger with something noxious-looking from a plastic squeeze bottle.

"Did you get it out?" he inquired hoarsely.

"Yes."

"Let me see."

"Are you sure you should?" Her voice carried stifled laughter, but she held out her mustard-stained hand for his inspection.

"Can't see a thing with that stuff all over it," he complained suspiciously. "Are you sure it's out?"

"It's out."

"What *is* that, anyway?"

"Iodine."

"Iodine? Whatever happened to nice antiseptic sprays in aerosol cans?"

"They're expensive. I use this for disinfecting the lambs' navels." Delilah blew on her finger to dry it and glanced sideways at him. "Tell me," she asked with amused curiosity, "how did you think you were going to be of any use to me around this place at lambing time if you faint at the first sign of blood?"

"Blood's got nothing to do with it," Luke said morosely, sitting up. "I can't stand inflicting pain on anyone. It's not my style." He smiled, then watched her face close and her eyes become guarded. It was as if, he thought in frustration, his smile had triggered an automatic defense mechanism.

As she turned from him to gather up the refuse from her most recent surgery, she said, "You don't have to worry about hurting me. I'm a lot tougher than I look."

"So you told me," he said, and then, unable to help himself, "Does *anything* ever get to you, 'Lilah."

She threw him that mulish look, and with some effort he dampened his own irritation. Cautiously and gently he probed, feeling his way. "Has any*one* ever gotten to you? Hurt you? Is that why you're so defensive?"

She gave him a flat stare. "I'm not defensive."

"The hell you're not."

She was looking down and away, but he could still see the pink tinge across her cheekbones. "Well, if I *am* defensive, maybe it's because this is none of your business."

"Ah-hah," he said, softly triumphant.

"Ah-hah *what*?"

With a small sense of victory he noted that he'd managed to rattle her. She'd lifted her head to fix him with a glare of disdain, but the look in her eyes was pure panic. Suddenly, irrelevantly, but not for the first time, he thought, Damn, she was beautiful. And, he reminded himself, she had the personality of Geronimo and the living habits of a hard-rock miner!

But then a vision touched him, shimmering with spring sunshine—her meadow, knee-deep in grass and abloom with daisies, and Delilah running toward him in slow motion, wearing that pink thing with the narrow straps and the lace across the top and bottom that he'd hung on the line this morning. . . .

Okay, maybe not Geronimo.

"Ah-hah," he repeated, so quietly it was more thought than whisper. "Someone's gotten to you." He was touching her, just his fingers on her cheek, and he couldn't recall ever having been so keyed to his sense of touch before. It was a shock to feel her warmth, to feel the way she seemed almost to melt into his skin. His fingertips slid across her cheek, counting and memorizing every pore, every microscopic irregularity. He brushed the wisps of hair that curled over the delicate shell of her ear, then followed the hairline down to the nape of her neck. Her eyes had a glazed look and her lips were slightly parted. He had an urge to kiss her that was like an ache demanding to be rubbed. *Don't be afraid of me*, he said silently. *I told you—hurting's not my style. . . .*

Her mouth was soft and fragrant, vibrant with promise and warm with banked fires, everything a woman's mouth should be. His mouth moved to hers and over hers, and into hers, a slow and tender melding that did nothing to disturb the fragility of her response. But instead of soothing his ache, it only made it worse, and when at last he pulled away, he had to swallow that ache before he could whisper, "See what I mean? That didn't hurt, did it?"

But even as he said it, he knew it wasn't true. He didn't know what it was doing to her, but it hurt him like *hell*. Making love to a beautiful woman was supposed to give—had always given—joy. Pleasure. At the very least, a bit of harmless fun. It wasn't supposed to make him burn from his Adam's apple to his groin like one big exposed nerve. He wanted to kiss her again and go on kissing her—every part of her—but something was keeping him from doing it. He didn't understand.

His fingers were nestled in the soft hair at her neck; the palm of his hand cradled her nape. When he removed his hand it felt like an amputation. After a long tense moment, during which she seemed to be holding her breath, he said, keeping his voice determinedly light, "Before you get mad and fire me for insubordination, consider that a kiss 'to make it better.' " He smiled at her, pleased that he could sound so cool and unruffled. "I couldn't kiss your finger because of all that iodine." He got to his feet and held out his hand. "Come on, let's finish your runway."

She jerked her eyes to his face and her lips parted as if she wanted to say something important. He waited, but she tightened her mouth and shook her head, accepting his offer of a hand up.

He thought she was unusually quiet as they worked together to nail the last planks into place. Her buoyant mood had gone flat, and Luke was sorry. He wasn't sure whether to blame the fact that he'd kissed her or the fact that she was obviously going to have to swallow a hefty portion of crow over the runway issue—although the Delilah he knew was more apt to be upset by the prospect of defeat than by a simple kiss! The funny thing was, though, he didn't care about scoring a victory anymore. He just wanted to give her this thing. A gift. Something to make her life a little easier. And, he thought confidently, that wounded pride of hers would stop twinging once that first ewe stepped through the holding-pen gate and headed down that runway, straight as an arrow to the barn door.

"There. Not a bad afternoon's work." Luke stood back to survey the finished job. Not bad at all, he thought. "Shall we give it a trial run?" he suggested. He felt like a little kid at Disneyland, and could barely conceal his excitement.

Delilah was hanging back, looking, Luke thought with tender amusement, almost apprehensive. "Luke . . ."

He smiled encouragingly down at her. "Come on, Blue Eyes. I'll let you do the honors."

Her face was set, tense. She really wasn't taking the defeat well at all, he thought, but he could understand how she felt. Some people just had a hard time facing the idea that they could be wrong.

"Go ahead," he urged her with a victor's generosity. "Let's see if it works."

Delilah gave him one last look of stony acceptance, lifted her shoulders in a helpless shrug, and moved to unwire the gate at the pen end of the runway. When she moved into the midst of the flock and began shooing them toward the gate, Luke stepped back, arms folded expectantly, to watch.

A ewe stepped into the runway, followed hesitantly by

several more. The rest of the flock was bunched around the bottleneck at the small opening.

The first ewe started down the narrow corridor, followed by a lengthening line of her sisters and cousins. When she saw the dark rectangle of the barn door yawning ahead she balked, and tried to turn back. But the runway was just wide enough to permit the one-way, single-file progress of a very pregnant ewe. She couldn't turn around, and she couldn't back up, not with her sisters and cousins all jammed in behind her.

The first ewe had only two choices, and she made hers without a moment's hesitation. Before Luke's astonished eyes she dropped to her knees and squeezed her impossible bulk *under* the bottom-most plank. In another moment she was trotting across the orchard—closely followed by about thirty other ewes.

As the dust was settling, Luke heard a strangled sound, and turned, speechless, to see Delilah standing all alone in the empty holding pen. One arm was wrapped across her middle; the other hand was clamped tightly over the lower half of her face. Over it her eyes stared at him, wide and bright with distress. And then she began to laugh—soundlessly and helplessly, the way she'd laughed when Luke had routed her amorous neighbor. Tears ran down her cheeks, and she doubled over, hugging herself and trying to catch her breath.

Luke was too stunned and too hurt to wait for her to give voice to her triumph with a gleeful whoop. He turned on his heel and strode across the orchard, ignoring both sheep and tree branches, making for the nearest fence. He vaulted it with gratifying ease and stalked around the corner of the barn. A minute later he was retrieving the missing component to the Incredible Hulk's distributor from under the straw in his bedroom stall.

A few more minutes after that, in a blind rage and without a thought for his credibility or personal safety, he was rocketing down the mountain toward the desert floor, toward the lights of town and the warmth and comradeship of *men*.

After she heard the pickup start and roar away, Delilah's laughter evaporated like desert rain, leaving the tears on her cheeks to dry more slowly. She hadn't meant to laugh, she thought. She *hadn't*.

She hadn't wanted to hurt him. Not since . . . *No*. Forget that kiss. It hadn't meant anything. Not since, then, he'd fainted over her injured finger. *I can't stand inflicting pain*, he'd said. *It's not my style.* . . . Well, it wasn't her style, either. Or never had been, until now. What was the matter with her? She'd never been a cruel person, and yet she'd hurt him. Hurt him unforgivably. She felt small, and sad, and a little bit scared, as if she might have let something important slip away. . . .

At least, she reflected with bitter irony as she called Lady to help round up the sheep and return them to the holding pen, she wouldn't have to worry about getting rid of Luke anymore. Not even someone as persistent as he would want to stick around after this!

Why didn't that thought make her feel any better?

It never occurred to Delilah to wonder how he'd managed to start her pickup so easily. It seemed entirely natural to her that any engine should fire under Luke MacGregor's masterful touch.

For the second night in a row Delilah finished her chores by flashlight. Afterward she carried the bucket of goat's milk into the house and made herself a sandwich out of what was left of the ham. She ate it leaning against the sink and staring unhappily at nothing. It didn't taste nearly as good as it had at lunchtime, in the orchard, with Luke. . . .

He'd be back, she told herself. Of course he'd be back. He wouldn't steal her truck. Who'd want it? And besides, he'd left some things here. Most notably, his airplane.

It seemed very quiet, and very lonely. How can you miss someone you'd never even heard of until the day before yesterday? she wondered.

She sighed, drank a glass of milk, and picked up her

flashlight. It had been too late to try to put any of the ewes into the barn tonight, but it wasn't too early to give them a final check before bedtime.

The sheep in the holding pen were placidly bedding down for the night. Deildah walked among them, shining the light on first one and then another, looking for the telltale signs of imminent labor: unusual restlessness, pawing the ground, an animal standing off by itself away from the flock. All was quiet. All seemed normal. She made one pass across the upper pasture with the flashlight's powerful beam and turned to go.

Then she stopped and made another sweep. In that brief moment's illumination something had jolted her awareness, something not quite right. Something out of the ordinary. She probed the darkness with the beam, stabbing at the abstract bulk of the disabled plane. There it was—a woolly gray lump. One ewe, all alone, in the shelter of the orange airplane. One ewe, standing off from the rest.

Delilah's heart began to beat faster. "Oh, damn," she murmured, and climbed the fence. Moving cautiously, not wanting to startle the animal, she started up the hill. She was still a good fifteen feet away when the ewe, who had been furiously pawing at the pasture stubble, suddenly dropped to her knees, then flopped onto her side.

Delilah swore softly. She knew who it was now. She'd recognized the purple ear tag and arrogant Roman nose. Number 907, and she was in the advanced stages of labor. Delilah trained the light on the ewe's hindquarters, and went cold all over. "Oh . . . no," she whispered, and tried not to panic.

In the flashlight beam she could plainly see one slippery black head and two forefeet—and that was good. But just as plain to see was a second set of feet, soft little white hooves facing upward. *Hind feet.* Baby lambs managed to get themselves incredibly tangled, and often turned around, while trying to be born, but there was only one explanation for an arrangement like this: Two lambs were in the birth canal at the same time. The backward twin was blocking the birth of the headfirst one. There was no way of telling how long the ewe had been struggling, but it didn't look good for the lambs' survival.

Delilah's shoulders sagged with the weight of frustration and futility. This was exactly the kind of thing she'd gone to the trouble and expense of building a barn for. In the confines of a clean stall she could have controlled the ewe and attempted to rearrange the lambs, but out here in the open, with an animal as big and wild as 907 . . .

Oh, if only Luke were there!

The ewe was still down, and obviously tiring. Delilah knew she had to try to do something, and it was now or never. Setting the flashlight on the ground, she darted to the ewe's side, gripped the upper foreleg, and folded it tightly against the animal's flank. By leaning her own weight onto the ewe's side, she could keep her pinned down. But all her efforts to push the lambs back to where there would be room to maneuver them into a single-file arrangement were being frustrated by the powerful contractions of the ewe's body. Delilah just wasn't strong enough to hold down the mother *and* manage the lambs by herself.

She was sobbing and swearing, and sweat was running down her face to mix with the tears of despair. When she heard her pickup groan and clatter to a stop, then the truck door slam, something surged inside her. "Luke," she whimpered, and then louder, "Luke!"

But the door to the house had already banged shut. He hadn't heard her. She sobbed in desperation. "Luke, damn you, I *need* you. *Please* come. . . ."

And then, miraculously, the door slammed one more time, and his voice came, calling, " 'Lilah, are you out there? 'Lilah?"

Summoning all her strength, she lifted her head from the ewe's heaving flank and shouted, "Up here—by the plane. I . . . need . . . you!" Then she collapsed, breathing in gulps, and whispering, "Please hurry, please hurry. . . ."

There was the thump of running footsteps, and the erratic zigzag of a flashlight's beam, and then Luke was beside her in the night.

"Here," Delilah said, and folded his strong hand around 907's foreleg. "Hold on tight." She began to explain in breathless gasps as she worked. "There's two . . . at once. Can't . . . push them . . . *back*. Got to . . . get this one . . . out of the *way*. . . . There! I think . . . I think I can . . . get it now—"

In the next instant a very long, very slippery, and very limp black bundle was sprawling in the rough pasture stubble. Delilah began to work quickly and frantically, wiping away the mucous that was clogging breathing passages, massaging and slapping the limp body.

"Here," she croaked, pulling her sweat shirt off and rubbing the lamb's head with it. "Take over. Never mind the mother, she's not going anywhere now. I've got to get that backward lamb out of there before it drowns."

"Is this one—?"

"I don't *know*. Don't give up. Pick it up by the hind feet and swing it back and forth—*hard*, like you're about to lob it over the fence, only *don't let go*. Luke," she begged with a sob when he still hesitated, staring at her as if she'd lost her mind, "*please*. No questions. Just do it, please!"

In less than a minute she had the second lamb, and, after a quick wipe of its face and nose, was swinging it like a giant pendulum, letting gravity and centrifugal force work to clear and stimulate the infant lungs. After a moment she felt some tension in the hind legs, and lowered the lamb quickly to the ground. There was a raspy gurgle, a rattly indrawn breath, and then a wet slapping noise as the lamb shook its head, setting its long ears to flapping.

"This one's gonna make it," she said in a low, tense voice. "How are you doing?"

There was silence. Delilah waited, swallowing a throatful of tears. Luke's voice came from out of the darkness, full of wonder. "It's sucking my finger. I guess that means it's all right, huh?"

"Yes." Delilah laughed softly, and then suddenly was crying and laughing at the same time. "We did it. I don't believe it. We did it, Luke, we saved them, both of them." She was sobbing and shaking, and her teeth were chattering.

Luke trained his flashlight on her. "Good lord, you're freezing. Where's your shirt?"

Delilah looked down at herself, belatedly realizing that the only thing between her and the frosty night air was a blue satin chemise with champagne lace trim. "On the lambs," she said jerkily, hunching her shoulders and trying to shrink away from the light.

The light moved, becoming a stationary slash across the pasture stubble. She heard Luke swear, then heard the metallic rasp of a zipper. Warmth enveloped her—the intimate warmth of Luke's body heat trapped in the fibers of his flight jacket. Still softly swearing, he pulled her back against his chest and tugged the edges of his jacket around to encompass them both.

Delilah protested, but the chattering of her teeth made it no more than an inarticulate whimper. "Hush," Luke whispered, and settled her more comfortably between his thighs. "What now?" he asked, wrapping his arms firmly across her chest.

What now, indeed? she wondered. She didn't feel cold anymore, but she just couldn't stop shaking. She couldn't think. She couldn't, absolutely couldn't, relax. She could only hold herself rigid while wave after wave of shivers coursed through her body.

As if in answer to Luke's question, number 907 suddenly lurched to her feet, and a moment later Delilah and Luke heard the soft, sticky sounds of mothering. Delilah sighed, and managed a low, unsteady laugh. "Nothing," she murmured.

"Nothing?"

"Right this minute. We'll let her get acquainted with the lambs, so she'll know they're hers. Then, when we pick them up and carry them to the barn, she'll follow."

"So for now we just sit here and wait?"

"Uh-huh."

" 'Lilah," he whispered, touching the outer rim of her ear with his lips, "You're cold."

"N-no, I'm . . . n-not. Really. I—"

"Then why are you still shaking?"

"I don't . . . *know*," she said jerkily. "Reaction, I guess."

Luke's voice was gruff. "I know, I know." He shifted his arms to hold her even more tightly. She felt the roughness of his jaw against the side of her neck, just below her ear, and a violent tremor rocketed through her.

"Come on, babe," he said, laughing a little. "Relax, now. . . ." The movement of his lips felt like kisses on the sensitive shell of her ear.

"I'm trying," she said in a very small voice, and closed her eyes. Seconds ticked away. She could feel his heart beating against her back.

"I don't believe it," Luke said suddenly in a voice taut with amazement. "Are they trying to stand up already?"

Delilah opened her eyes and laughed, relieved at the diversion. "Yeah," she breathed, lifting a hand to wipe at her cheeks. "Aren't they something?"

"They sure are. And you know what else?" His voice had a certain focused intensity that puzzled her. She half-turned in his arms, lifting her face to look for his in the cold starry darkness.

Luke's hand framed her face, his thumb touching one cheekbone, his fingertips the other. Very slowly he traced the line of her jaw, clear down to her chin. "So," he muttered fiercely, "are you." And then he kissed her.

Seven

It was what she'd wanted, what she'd been wanting all afternoon, ever since he'd kissed her in the barn. That wasn't something she knew with conscious thought, but with something far more primitive and uncontrollable. Something that exulted in wild triumph as Luke's mouth closed over hers. Something that exploded in her belly with a painful, dizzying lurch. As her head fell back in full surrender, she made a small, desperate sound and clutched at the arm that lay across her ribs.

Luke made a sound, too, deep-throated and hungry. His mouth shifted. Hers opened, accepting a deeper joining. His hand was warm on her throat. It moved slowly downward, and, finding nothing to impede it, slipped inside the lacy top of her chemise. Her breasts were full and tight with yearning. His hand brushed across one taut nipple, then gently, oh, so gently, cupped the other breast, cradling it tenderly, as if he knew just how terribly it ached. . . .

But while Luke's hand was gentle, his mouth was not. What she had willingly surrendered he plundered without mercy, his tongue driving deep and with an evocative rhythm that left her incapable of thought and bereft of will. Her body was on fire. She didn't feel the cold anymore, or the rough ground. Forgotten were the two tiny miracles struggling to find their own spindly legs and take their first tottering steps. She'd never been kissed like this before. It was . . . mastery. Dominance. Sexual possession, pure and simple. It probed deep into her core and found all her hidden pockets of desire and released them to build pressures in her that terrified her. . . .

She began to struggle, not of her own volition, but in a panic born of an instinct for self-preservation. Luke released her mouth, but didn't move his hand. Beneath it her chest heaved, each breath a stabbing, searing pain.

"Please . . ." she whispered. "Don't . . ."

He lowered his head and touched his lips to her throat, then opened his mouth and sought the hollow at its base with his tongue. Delilah arched and moaned softly. Luke lifted his head just long enough to murmur, "Why not?"

"Because—" she said with a croak, and couldn't go on. He was interfering with her voice box, her breathing. She managed to free a hand from the flight jacket and insert it between his mouth and her neck. He laughed and kissed her palm, then straightened, holding her captive, cradled in his arms. She looked up at him, a dark shape against stars, and whispered, "I don't *know* you."

" 'Lilah . . ." His voice had that mesmerizing hum. "You've seen me asleep—unconscious. You've put stitches in me, nursed me, undressed me, washed my clothes. We've eaten breakfast together, worked together, laughed and quarreled together. I've driven your truck, hung up your underwear—*Hush*," he said, holding her more tightly when she tried to pull away, "—and kissed you. More than once. And," he added in a low, intimate growl, "we both enjoyed it a lot. If we knew each other any better—"

"Two days," Delilah said. "It's been *two days*."

Luke exploded. "What's time got to do with it? 'Lilah, we never were strangers!"

The words rang in the night air. She struggled to a sitting position, and he let her go. So he had felt it, too, she thought, that instant intimacy she found so disconcerting. Why was it so difficult to deal with? Why was she fighting him so hard when every nerve and cell in her body was responding to him as if tuned to his wavelength? It couldn't be fear of rejection, an old, old goblin of hers. He was pursuing *her*. It shouldn't be that she was afraid of getting hurt. She didn't *want* anything permanent or encumbering anyway. Did she? She was a grown woman and he was . . . devastatingly attractive. Simply a matter of sex. Why was she so afraid?

" 'Lilah," he said with quiet frustration, "what do you want me to do? Call you up and ask for a date?" He waited a moment, then gave an exasperated little laugh. "You don't even have a phone! You want to go to a movie? Make out in the back seat of the car?" Another pause, and then a clicking sound as he snapped his fingers. "Damn. I forgot you don't have a back seat. Well . . ."

She shook her head, and then, afraid he wouldn't be able to see the motion, made a muffled sound of denial. "That's not what I mean!"

" 'Lilah," he persisted gently, "I don't know whether it was fate or accident that landed me in your pasture—"

"I don't believe in fate."

"Accident, then. Accidents happen. Should we ignore what's happening, just because we didn't plan it? We're not kids, 'Lilah. Do we really have to play the games kids play?"

"I never liked games," she murmured, lifting her chin slightly.

"Well, then? If I know what I want, and you—"

"But I *don't*. I don't know what I want!"

He was silent for a moment, and in the cold darkness Delilah started to shiver again. One of the newborn lambs began to bump its nose along her back, searching for nourishment. She steered it back toward its mother and sniffled loudly.

"Okay," Luke said softly. "Fair enough. I'll wait . . . until you do know."

The misguided lamb was back, persistently bumping her elbow, her ribs. "Dummy," she muttered, and gathered the sopping-wet baby into her arms. Over its head she glared at the dark shape that was Luke MacGregor and blurted out the question that had been there all along, in the back of her mind. "Why?"

She waited breathlessly for his answer, for something glib, flattering, wooing, winning. . . . But instead there was a moment's hesitation and then rueful laughter. "Damned if I know," he said finally. She heard a whispery sound, as if he were rubbing his hands over his face. "Except that . . ." The laughter in his voice was now almost tender. "Except that you . . . are one hell of a lady. You mystify me, Delilah Beaumont. You infuriate me. You fascinate me . . . excite me. . . . Shall I go on?"

"No," she muttered, swallowing hard and trying to contain the tremors inside her. She felt inexplicably weak, and scared. "Just . . . please, help me get the lambs to the barn."

"Anything you say, boss," Luke said with soft intensity. "If there's anything you need, I'll be here. Because I intend to stick around until you wake up and realize just what it is you really want. . . ."

After talking with Pete that night, Luke sat in his plane, staring into the darkness.

Why? Delilah had asked him. That was a question only she would ask. She was one of a kind, and not his kind. She wasn't even his type. He liked his women long, blond, and uncomplicated, sunny golden girls with laughter in their eyes and awareness in the way they moved.

This one was small, dark, and intense, and most of the time she acted about as sexy as Sitting Bull. And she fascinated him . . . and more. He couldn't believe how much he wanted her. Was she beautiful? Funny, he didn't even know anymore. All he saw when he looked at her now was . . . Delilah. The truth of it was, he just wanted *her*, and what she looked like didn't have much to do with it.

She wasn't what he'd expected. This whole thing wasn't going the way he'd expected. It had never been a complicated thing before—wanting a woman—but this wanting had strings tied all over it, like a cat's cradle, and he couldn't tell what they were connected to or where they might lead.

He felt a flash of fear, like distant lightning, the same flicker he'd felt when he'd made the decision to put his plane down in her pasture. Once again he was afraid something was happening to him that he wasn't going to be able to control.

Delilah stirred, burrowing deeper under the Navaho rug she was using as a blanket. Bacon again? she wondered dimly. The smell was much stronger this time.

Something warm and coffee-scented brushed her cheek, then touched the tip of her nose—a silken promise. She opened her eyes to a landscape confusingly populated with odd fuzzy shapes in yellows and browns.

A voice drawled. " 'Mornin', sunshine."

The landscape swam into focus, becoming browned sausage links and slabs of French toast on a plate. Across it a pair of eyes stared into hers; eyes the color of fresh-brewed coffee. They had the same stimulating effect as a cup of coffee—Delilah's heart and nervous system shifted instantaneously into high gear. She gave an interrogative chirp, then cleared her throat and said incredulously, "Breakfast? In *bed*?"

Luke was sitting beside her on the bed. He balanced the plate on her stomach and looked around. "That was the idea, but I think it's colder in this room than it is in the barn." His eyes came back to her just as she was thinking, Dear Lord, he *was* beautiful. . . . She'd forgotten last night in the darkness just how beautiful he was. She coughed and eased one arm out from under the rug to poke cautiously at the glistening amber puddle in the middle of the French toast.

"Do you always sleep with all your clothes on?" he asked, frowning.

Delilah transferred the exploratory finger to her mouth. "Real maple syrup," she said, and sighed, closing her eyes. Why, Luke? she asked silently. Why was he doing this to her?

"Here, try a fork." Luke's voice had a smile in it, as his fingers gently closed around her wrist. In the midst of licking syrup from her lips she opened her eyes and caught him watching the movement of her tongue with a look that could only be described as hungry. Last night came back on a tidal wave of sensual memory. Her lips, tingling with cooling moisture, suddenly felt swollen and exposed.

Luke seemed . . . different this morning, she mused. There were lines around his mouth she hadn't noticed before, and the skin under his eyes looked fragile and bruised, as if he hadn't been sleeping well. It was more than that, though. It was something in his eyes, the way he looked at her. Something she'd missed last night in the dark. He wasn't frowning, not exactly. It was more a kind of intensity that hadn't been there yesterday, even when he'd kissed her in the barn. Before last night, when he'd kissed her she'd had the impression he was playing a game, one he'd played many times before and was very, very good at. One he enjoyed, but didn't take very seriously. She knew that if he kissed her now it wouldn't be a game. . . .

He didn't kiss her. She wondered whether the queer little lurch in her stomach was relief or disappointment. Instead he held both her hands and said, "Up," and pulled until she was sitting upright in bed, with the plate teetering precariously on her knees. That brought her so close to him, she could feel the heat radiating from his body. Her bedroom didn't seem cold at all to her, and she noticed that Luke hadn't mentioned it again, either.

They both realized suddenly that he was still holding her hands. She moved to reclaim them, but he changed his grip, turned her hands palm up, and began stroking his thumbs across her palms.

Unexpectedly he murmured, "How do they stay so soft?" and turned his own hands up so she could see the blisters and calluses. "The work you do . . ."

His hands, she thought. He'd ruined them, building her a sheep run, and she had laughed.

She made a soft, unconscious sound of sympathy and covered his ravaged hands with her own. Their roughness pricked at her skin and sent jagged little currents into her arms. She couldn't seem to break the contact, though he wasn't holding her.

"Um . . . it's the sheep," she said huskily.

"The sheep?"

"Didn't you know? Working with sheep keeps your hands soft."

"How does working with sheep keep your hands soft?" He was smiling again, his eyes crinkly and indulgent. Yesterday his attitude would have set off temper flares, but now all she could do was say with a croak, "Lanolin."

"Lanolin?" He was lightly stroking her forearms, nudging the sleeves of her sweat shirt upward, out of the way. The roughness of his hands continued to send out advance patrols that made sneak attacks on her nerves.

"Didn't you know?" she asked, her voice rushed and breathy. "Lanolin comes from sheep's wool."

"Fascinating . . ."

His hands had reached her elbows. Her own hands were resting on the insides of his forearms, just below the elbows. He felt warm, and smooth, and firm. "Of course," she said, giving her head a desperate shake, "it doesn't work for anything but hands—" His thumbs were gently massaging the inner bend of her elbows.

"Why not?"

"Well, because . . . You have to *touch* it." She stopped, coughed, and knew she was blushing. The sensual image of herself rolling naked on a sheepskin rug as a routine part of her nightly schedule was just too much. And Luke's eyes were very bright and carried strange, golden lights. Delilah had an idea he might be sharing her fantasy, but he merely nodded gravely and said, "Of course."

He picked up the wobbling plate and took the fork from her hand, using it to carve out a bite-sized section of toast. "Breakfast," he said placidly. "Come on, open up."

Delilah was still rattled enough to follow orders. After a moment she managed to mutter crossly, "It's *cold*."

"Since when has that bothered you? Ready for another bite?"

"No! I don't—"

He gave her a beatific smile and murmured, "Tweet, tweet, here comes the mama bird. . . ."

Delilah shocked herself by erupting in a fit of giggles. She *never* giggled. She clamped a hand over her mouth to keep the offending sounds in and the "mama bird's" offering out. "MacGregor," she protested, "you're not going to sit here and feed me!"

Luke paused, eyebrows raised and fork poised. "Why not?"

Why not? she repeated silently. Because it made her throat close just to look at him. Because . . .

"You—you make me nervous!"

A slow, exultant smile warmed his eyes, and he lowered the fork. "Why," he purred in his wooing voice, "do I make you nervous?"

Why? Oh, dear Lord.

Because she was nervous, she blurted out what was in her mind. "Because you're too beautiful!"

Luke made a strangled coughing noise and abruptly leaned over to set the breakfast plate on the floor. Delilah was sorry to see it go. It had been a distraction, at least, and a barrier of sorts between them. Now she felt imperiled, like a helpless creature suddenly deprived of its protective coloring in the presence of the predator.

Luke cleared his throat, folded his arms across his chest, regarded her with a wary frown, and said, "I'm too *what*?"

His tan had deepened, acquired a dusky cast. Delilah wondered with amazement if he could possibly be blushing. That idea was so intriguing that it bolstered her courage, and since it was too late to retract anyway, she repeated the idiotic statement. "Beautiful. You know, as in handsome. Good looking." He continued to regard her with unblinking gravity—rather, she thought, like a miffed owl. With a touch of asperity she added, "Well, it must have occurred to you that you *are*."

He cleared his throat again and rubbed his hand over the back of his neck as if he didn't know quite what else to do with it. And with each manifestation of his discomfort, a funny little warm spot in the vicinity of Delilah's heart shivered and grew.

His frown deepened, as if he were trying hard to understand her. "And that bothers you?"

"Yes," she said staunchly. "It does. I'm sorry, I can't help it."

"You mean," he said slowly, "that you'd be more comfortable with me if my eyes were a little smaller and my nose a little bigger and my ears stuck out?"

"Well," she hedged, while her eyes defied her by feasting on his offending face. Then she gave up, closed her eyes, and moaned, "Ye-es . . ."

He was touching her face, measuring her features with his fingers, tracing the line of her brows, brushing the tips of her eyelashes, stroking her cheek with the backs of his fingers, and finally drawing his thumb across her lower lip. She held herself very still, wanting to lean into his touch and all the more determined not to.

"What do you see when you look in the mirror, Blue Eyes?"

She looked at him. "I don't know." Her words pushed her lips against his fingers. "Just . . . me, I guess."

"Me too." His smile was just slightly askew. She found it every bit as endearing as his blush, and even more potent an assault on her resistance than the angel's smile or the puckish grin. "And a few centimeters more or less don't have much to do with who I am."

Every cliché she'd ever heard told her he was right. *Beauty is only skin-deep. . . . Pretty is as pretty does.* . . . But deep in her heart she didn't believe a word of it. He'd had that face all his life, been treated differently in certain subtle ways because of it. Had women falling all over themselves to please him because of it. No wonder he thought he could drop into her life, literally out of the blue, and take control of every single aspect of it without a struggle. *I'll wait,* he'd said with unshakable self-confidence. No wonder.

"But I don't know who you are," she protested feebly.

His hand was moving again, fingers just barely skimming the surface of her skin, stirring nerve endings like a breath of warm air, exploring her jawline, the shape of her ear, the taut cords of her neck, and the delicate hollows below throat and collarbone.

"You could know me," he was saying, "if you'd let yourself. . . ."

"Don't," she said suddenly, shivering.

"Don't what?"

His hand had reached her shoulder, and almost casually he began to move the material of her sweat shirt back and forth over her skin. She shrugged, trying unsuccessfully to dislodge his hand. "Don't do *that.* You're always . . . touching me."

"And you don't like that?"

"Right!"

"Wrong. And that's what bothers you, isn't it, Blue Eyes?" He was leaning forward, smiling, relaxed and irritatingly confident. But there was something in his eyes that held hers, and kept her silent. "You like it too much. I know because of this"—his finger touched one hot cheek—"and this"—he traced the fullness of her lower lip. "And because I can see it in your eyes."

Delilah moaned helplessly and flopped back on her pillow, pulling the rug up over her head. From under it she shouted, "Cut it out, MacGregor, or I swear—" Muffled laughter touched her, and then his warm presence was gone from her side, leaving a curious void. How could he sit there and say he hadn't been affected by that face? she thought furiously. Of all the conceited, overconfident, arrogant . . . Thinking he'd gone, she threw back the rug.

He was standing in the doorway, leaning against the frame. "One more thing, boss," he drawled, taking in her rumpled and flushed appearance with cool amusement. "You might take a good long look at your motives for putting me out there in that barn—"

"My motives! It seems pretty—"

"Irrational," Luke finished with maddening calm. "Considering you don't have enough blankets to cover your own bed because of it."

"Irrational! After last night? When every time I turn around you—you try to kiss me? You're lucky I'm even letting you stay around!"

"*Try* to kiss you?" The words were very soft, but something kindled in his eyes—a warning, and a reminder. Remembering where she was, Delilah bit back her fury and tore her gaze from his face. She'd never felt so vulnerable, so at a disadvantage. It would be a grave mistake to challenge him. As her gaze fell on the plate of French toast lying forgotten and abandoned on the floor, she wondered if it would be as satisfying as she thought it might be to hurl it at his head. His gaze followed hers, then came back to her face. He shook his head slightly and smiled knowingly, making it very hard for her to resist the impulse. The only thing that stopped her was the awareness that she would probably miss, and then he would have the last laugh anyway.

She'd have to get more blankets, she thought when he had gone, leaving a chuckle hanging in the crisp air. But she never once thought, as a solution to her problem, of telling him to go. . . .

In their nice, warm stall in the barn the newborn lambs were nursing vigorously, tails aquiver. Delilah carefully set the hypodermic full of antibiotics on the plank that ran across the top of the stall gate and paused a moment just to watch. Luke came and stood behind her and put his hands on her shoulders. After one involuntary jolt she stood quite still.

Maybe she'd get used to it, she thought, having him touch her. It would be better if she didn't try to fight him. And it was much easier like this, with him behind her, out of sight. It was easier when she couldn't see his face.

He chuckled, his breath stirring her hair. "Cute little devils. Kept me awake all night."

She nodded, and thought, *I wish he'd kiss me again.* Thoughts were treacherous things. That one stunned and sobered her.

Luke didn't kiss her, and the lambs had satisfied their appetites for the moment. She picked up the syringe and went into the stall to treat Number 907 for possible aftereffects of precipitous and unsanitary lambing.

After the morning chores were done, she left Luke rearranging the haystack and went to town to borrow some blankets from Mara Jane Underwood. On the way down the mountain she met a flatbed truck carrying a trencher, a roll of fence wire, and what looked like some small miscellaneous building materials.

Oh, good, she thought. It looked like they were finally going to build that culvert at Deer Creek.

Eight

Over a cup of coffee at Mara Jane's, Delilah found herself confiding in her friend her mixed feelings for Luke MacGregor. Although Delilah wasn't used to feminine heart-to-heart talks, she felt somewhat better just for having talked with someone.

"If only he weren't so good-looking," Delilah said as she was leaving with an armload of blankets. "Do you have any idea what it's like to have somebody around all the time who it almost hurts to look at?"

"Just think of it as a physical handicap," Mara Jane advised. "Like a scar, or a deformity. I'll bet after a while you won't even notice."

The first thing Delilah saw when she returned was a narrow strip of freshly turned earth, as if a very large and determined mole had dug a beeline from the house to the barn. There was no sign of Luke, but from somewhere above the barn came the slightly syncopated rhythm of echoing hammer blows. Though the connection between the trencher she had seen on the flatbed truck and the giant mole-digging across her yard was obvious, there was no sign of that piece of equipment. It had done its job and departed. Remembering the roll of wire fencing that had also been on that truck, Delilah was pretty sure, even without the hammering sounds, where she would find Luke MacGregor.

A few minutes later she was leaning against the barn doorway overlooking the orchard, weak-kneed and shaking with silent, rueful laughter. She had told Mara Jane that Luke looked like the man on the cover of one of her books, and there he was, the hero of *Raven's Rapture* in the flesh.

The afternoon sun was warm, and, like that particular figment of Mara Jane's imagination, Luke was working without a shirt. But, unlike any paper hero, Luke MacGregor was firm, resilient flesh and warm blood. His body glistened with sweat. She knew he would smell of sun and earth and hard-working man. . . .

Delilah had a sudden impulse to turn and run. She dreaded being caught there, watching him. But it was already too late.

"Hi, boss." He was grinning at her, wiping his forehead with his arm. He drove another staple into a post, securing a section of wire fencing, and stood back to let her survey the finished run. "What do you think?"

What did she think? She couldn't think, she could only feel. She felt angry, confused, afraid, helpless, full of resentment, full of yearning . . .

Anger seemed safest. It tingled through her like static electricity, lifting the fine hairs on her skin and crackling in her voice. "What the hell do you think you're doing? I left you with a job to do."

He lifted his eyebrows at her, but only said mildly, "Haystack's all done. Straw bales all on the barn side of the stack, except for the two I put down in the clean stalls for bedding." He plucked his shirt from a tree limb and came toward her, tossing the shirt casually over his shoulder. Again Delilah had to resist an urge to bolt. When he stopped just a step away from her, so close that she could see the tiny drops of sweat among the dark hairs on his chest and feel the heat of his exertion, she thought wildly that she'd never get used to this—never!

"What did you—" She stopped, swallowed, and began again. "Did you *buy* all this stuff?" Dear Lord, where could she look? Certainly not at his face—his eyes were promises in brown velvet, his mouth a sensual reminder. The lines of his neck and shoulders were over-poweringly masculine, evocative of some proud and virile animal—a stallion, or a stag. He wasn't a big man, but he seemed to radiate almost palpable power and energy. It left her feeling cowed. Weak. She fought it, desperately clinging to her anger and her authority. "How could you spend money without my authorization? I told you I can't—"

"It's my money," he said easily, folding brawny arms across his naked chest and regarding her from under half-closed eyelids.

"It's my place, dammit!"

"Consider it a loan." She caught the glitter of his eyes through his lashes, but couldn't tell whether he was angry or amused. "I expect to be paid back—with interest."

"Don't you think you should *ask* me first?" She was shouting, really shouting, angrier than she could ever remember being in her life. "I don't *want* a loan. I can't afford interest! I can't afford *you*! I want you out of here—out of my life! And what the hell did you do to my driveway? I don't—"

He moved quickly. Tucking the hammer into the waistband of his jeans, he took her by the arms, spun her around, and marched her back into the barn.

He *was* angry, she thought. She could feel it in the controlled violence of his movements, and in the ruthlessness of his fingers on her upper arms. Why hadn't she noticed that ruthlessness and violence before? For the first time her vague fears took on form and became reasonable. Who *was* this man? She didn't know him. He could be a maniac. He could be—he *was* a brute. He'd just been hiding his true nature behind that angel's smile and devil's charm. . . .

They had crossed the barn. As they approached the front door, Luke suddenly spun her back around and pinned her firmly against the wall with one hand on her shoulder. She shrank involuntarily and closed her eyes.

"Open your eyes," he said harshly, "and I'll show you what I did to your driveway."

There was a soft click. She opened her eyes, but even suspecting what she was going to see couldn't prevent one shocked gasp from escaping. The barn was flooded with light—cool blue fluorescent light from a six-foot fixture firmly mounted under the ceiling's center beam. From the fixture a professional-looking metal conduit snaked across the beam and down the cement-block wall to a metal switch box at her left shoulder. And that wasn't all. Running the length of the side walls, along the back of the stalls just above the level of the fences, was an outlet bar with electrical plugs accessible to each and every stall.

Delilah opened her mouth, licked her lips, cleared her throat, then shook her head, utterly speechless.

"The cable is underground," Luke said, sounding as if he were gritting his teeth. "It connects to your main fuse-box. You can turn it off from there if you choose not to use it."

She shook her head again. Impotent rage had boiled through her with a surge of adrenaline that left her weak, trembling, drained. "You did . . . all this . . . this morning?" she whispered finally.

"When I was in town last night I ran into your friend Roy Underwood," he said. "I wrote out the order for the materials, and he dropped it off at the lumber yard for me this morning."

"Why, Luke?" She lifted her gaze to his face. The look in his eyes was one she'd never seen there before—narrow and intense, and filled with an anger as fierce as her own. "Why did you do this?"

"*Why?*" His anger ignited and took off like a rocket. "Why the hell do you always have to ask why! You put me out here in this damn barn with no heat and no lights. I wanted a place to plug in my electric blanket, okay?" He braced a hand against the block wall beside her head. To Delilah he seemed to loom over her, an erupting Vesuvius. His voice lowered, became tense and gravelly. "Dammit, Delilah, do I have to have permission from you to do something nice? I just wanted—I wanted to do something for you. I wanted to help you. I owe you *something* for—"

"You don't owe me anything! I don't want your help! I don't need your help!"

"The hell you don't!"

"I don't . . . want . . . help. I have to make it on my own. Can't you get that through your thick head?"

They stared at each other, breathing hard, while their furious shouts echoed away into emptiness. Then Luke said softly, "I've got news for you. Nobody makes it alone. Nobody. 'No man is an island. . . .' "

Incensed, Delilah shot back recklessly, "Oh, bravo. But you know what they say, 'Even the devil quotes scripture for his purposes'!"

Luke gave a bark of triumphant laughter. "That's not scripture. Did you sleep through English Lit 1A? That's John Donne!"

"Oh, yeah? Well, here's one for you! 'I am a rock, I am—' "

"Simon and Garfunkel," he interrupted, then paused. "I think I understand," he said after a moment. "Isn't the rest of it something about a rock never feeling any pain"—he touched her chin and gently lifted it, forcing her to look at him—"and an island never crying?"

He didn't seem to move, yet somehow he was nearer, so close that she felt enveloped, suffocated. She said, "Let me go," in a voice she'd never used before, a husky voice, frightened, but with a strange, breathless element of excitement . . . or expectation. She wondered suddenly what had become of her anger, and his.

Except for the fingers beneath her chin, Luke wasn't touching her, and yet his body seemed to be pressing her back against the cold concrete. When he spoke she could almost feel the vibrations, as if the words were a direct transmission of energy, bypassing primitive human auditory mechanisms.

"It won't work, you know," he said. "Sometimes you have to feel pain. Sometimes you have to cry."

"Let . . . me . . . go."

"You're not an island, Delilah Beaumont," he drawled softly, curving his lips in a sweet, lazy smile. "You know how I know? Because you definitely need someone. You need *me*."

"You!" It was a desperate sound, a whispered explosion.

"Me. I know you don't want to believe that . . . so I'm going to have to prove it to you." His head moved, slowly descending.

"No," she choked out, and, jerking her chin from his grasp, lowered her head.

"Yes," he whispered, moving his hand down the side of her neck to rest lightly on her shoulder. With no more force than that he held her captive.

She closed her eyes and brought her hands up to his chest. It was a shock to feel his flesh beneath her palms, firm, warm, with a sensually intriguing texture of hair. It was a shock, too, to feel his heart hammering against her hand. It was so wild, its cadence so furious and untamed, it couldn't have any connection with *him*. He was an iceman—so calm, so damnably controlled. Slowly, unbearably slowly, his head descended. The tension grew, and became intolerable. Her heart was pounding as if it had a life of its own, and each breath felt like a sob, the dry, tearing sobs of nightmare.

And then his warm breath touched her cheek, her nose, her lips . . . and nothing more. His mouth just hung there, waiting, no more than a sigh away from hers. If she drew breath, if she spoke or sighed or moistened her lips, they would touch his, and then . . . What then?

The hand on her shoulder quivered. So faint a movement, but it relaxed her tension as simply as the clean release of the arrow relaxes the bow. Delilah made a small sound of frustration and need, and moved at last, parting her lips and raising her face to him in tentative surrender.

A chuckle, soft and intimate, stirred across her lips. His mouth, open and hungry, brushed hers so lightly, it tickled. She made a deep-throated, inarticulate protest.

He responded with a low murmur that could only be a question. Her fingers curled, unconsciously stroking, and her head moved, impatiently seeking. The sound that rumbled in his throat became a growl of masculine triumph.

She wanted him. Her body knew it, and made sure that her mind did too. She was filling up with a deep, shimmering heat, a kind of trembling incandescence. And she knew he knew it, too, and still he denied her. When she lifted her chin, gently urging, and caressed his lips with hers, he laughed softly, warming her mouth with his breath, but resisted her invitation to increase the contact beyond that tantalizing feather's touch.

She made another sound she'd never used before, a uniquely feminine growl of vexation. This time his answering chuckle was tender, not triumphant. His hand moved to cradle the back of her head and press her by slow, excruciating degrees into a deep and languid kiss. She sighed, the grateful sigh of a thirsty traveler taking a long, cool drink. . . .

And then, without haste but without warning, he left her. He simply lifted his head and stepped back. Her hands, no longer supported by his chest, fell limp at her sides. She swayed, and his hand shot out to grasp her elbow. She opened her eyes then, and, blinded by the unexpected fluorescence, stood blinking, disoriented and confused, like someone waking up in a strange place.

"There," Luke said huskily. "Now try to tell me you don't need me."

Delilah's lips felt stiff and cold. "You bas—" she began, but he silenced her with a finger laid firmly across her mouth.

"Ah-ah, careful. That's no way to talk to the man who's going to be your lover."

She drew breath for vehement denial, but he shook his head and lifted his finger to touch his own lips. "Shh . . ." he whispered. "One day." He blew her a kiss, smiled his angel's smile, and strolled down the barn's center aisle and out into the orchard.

Delilah noticed with a shock that the shirt he'd plucked from the tree branch still hung from the hook of his finger, over his shoulder and down his back. He'd beaten her, utterly devastated and humiliated her, almost literally with one hand behind him!

Luke strode through the orchard, vaulted the holding-pen fences without a thought, and kept going across the pasture until he reached the dubious haven of his wrecked plane. It was, he noticed, beginning to look a trifle forlorn and abandoned. He wondered how much longer he could get away with leaving it there like a broken toy discarded in the grass.

The chill breath of March swept across the pasture, but he didn't put his shirt on. Not yet. Lord knew he needed cooling off—though he didn't think even a blizzard could put out the fire in his loins.

He wasn't proud of himself; he didn't think he'd ever done a thing like that before. But then, he'd never known a woman like Delilah before. Had never met anyone, in fact, who had the power to make him lose his temper.

As he stood scowling at the listing airplane, the sun slipped behind the looming Sierra escarpment. At almost the same moment he heard Delilah's front door slam. Suddenly cold, he shrugged into his shirt and began to do up the buttons. His movements felt jerky and uncoordinated.

He thought morosely about calling Pete. But the radio batteries were probably dead. He'd have to call from town.

He squinted up at the snow-covered peaks, then glanced at his watch. Sundown came early on the Sierra's eastern slope. He probably had time for a quick run down the mountain. It was doubtful that Delilah would tolerate his help with the chores tonight anyway.

The truth was, he didn't feel much like talking to Pete.

He didn't want to think about court dates, or drilling moratoriums, or a bleeding-heart, bullheaded, reactionary judge named Andrew Beaumont!

He suddenly balled up his fist and brought it down hard on the metal skin of the plane's canted wing. Then he slowly flexed his fingers and rotated his head, easing the tension out of his neck and shoulders.

He'd call Pete . . . tomorrow.

That night the lambing began in earnest.

Nine

The sheep run was *there*, Delilah told herself. She had to use it. There was no other way of getting the sheep from the holding pen to the barn. She tied back the gate and herded the first of the most urgently expectant ewes through the opening.

At the far end of the run the barn's open doorway was rhinestone-bright against the dusk. The sight of it made her feel like crying. She couldn't rationalize away that swift surge of emotion that sent aches and tickles stinging through her nose and throat like a cloud of spring pollen.

What was the matter with her? she wondered. Why, oh, *why* this awful confusion of feelings? She was acting like . . . like a child in a tantrum, a child who, at her most unlovable, most wants to be loved. Was that what was the matter with her? Did she just want to be *loved*?

But, she thought, she wanted *this*. Her own place, her sheep. She'd worked so hard, given up so much.

What had Mara Jane said this morning? That she should follow her feelings. But exactly *what* feelings? Luke made her feel like rockets and shooting stars and every other cliché she could think of. And sometimes he made her feel soft and yielding, as if all her bones had melted. All right, she admitted silently. Yes, she was attracted to him! But that wasn't love. And he certainly didn't love *her*. So when Mara Jane spoke of feelings, what did she mean? Did she mean this melting, shimmering desire? Or love—the forever kind?

And what happened, she wondered in silent confusion as she gave 907 and her twins a final check and turned out the light, if she didn't want that kind of love, if she valued her independence too much?

On her way down to the house she met Luke, on his way up to the barn. He had a blanket rolled under his arm and a flashlight in his hand, and the sight of him was like a kick in the stomach.

"There's a pot of stew on the stove," he told her, his voice dry and casual. "I thought if things got hectic during the next few days, you might want something easy to heat up. Salad's in the fridge."

"Thanks," she acknowledged gruffly.

"Well," he said, switching on the flashlight, "see you in the morning."

"Yes . . . good night," she mumbled, and went up the steps, brushing angrily at something cold and wet on her cheeks. *I'm an island,* she thought bitterly as the comforting aroma of simmering beef stew enveloped her.

How ironic it was that while sharing her living quarters with another human being for the first time in nearly three years, she felt lonelier than she ever had in her life.

She set her alarm for midnight. When it went off, she waited for the adrenaline shock to ebb, then pulled her clothes on over her thermals. Her muscles felt weak and shaky, her brain stiff and muddy. No matter how many times her alarm woke her, no matter how many times she had to rouse herself out of a deep sleep and warm bed to venture out alone into a cold, dark night, it never seemed to get any easier. It was only manageable if she didn't allow herself to dwell on it.

The barn was warm and moist in spite of wide-open windows. It was full of the stirrings and rumblings of twenty placidly masticating sheep . . . and, like a counter-rhythm to the night symphony, the soft breathing sounds Luke made as he slept.

Delilah didn't turn on the light. For the first few minutes she managed to keep herself from invading his privacy with the flashlight. After one cursory sweep over the flock and a brief check of 907 and her twins, though, her flashlight beam seemed drawn to that first stall on the left as if by a magnet.

It had to be love, she thought wryly. He even looked beautiful when he slept.

The thought slipped into her conscious mind without warning, shaking her so badly, she nearly dropped the flashlight. *No!* she shouted silently, and tried to look away from the man who lay as obliviously asleep in her hay as Little Boy Blue. She couldn't, though. She tried to justify the avid way her gaze clung to his face by attempting to discern some flaw in him. Just one unappealing detail. She couldn't do that, either.

He lay on his back, one arm thrown out wide, the other bent at the elbow to cradle his head. The blankets that covered him stopped just short of his armpits. Above them his arms and shoulders were bare. As she watched the gentle rise and fall of his chest, Delilah wondered what might happen if she were to lie down on the straw-cushioned blankets and stretch her body out alongside his, pillow her head on the hollow of his shoulder, turn her face to his chest, and taste the sweet-salt tang of his skin with her tongue. . . .

Behind her there was a sudden scuffling as a heavy-burdened ewe settled awkwardly onto the barn's concrete floor. Delilah jerked the flashlight to the spot, guilt making her heart thump like a kettledrum. But the ewe's legs were doubled comfortably under her and she was placidly chewing her cud, watching Delilah with an opaque and unblinking regard. Delilah sighed, cast the light once more across the rest of the flock, and turned to go.

" 'Lilah," Luke murmured, his voice sleepy-groggy and husky, "what time is it?"

She gripped the door for support and croaked out, "A little past midnight, I think. I don't have a wrist-watch. . . ."

" 'S okay. When's the next watch?"

"Um . . . three should be fine."

"I'll take it."

"You don't have an alarm—"

"Got my watch. Shine the light here a minute."

Delilah had to brace the light on the top of the gate to keep it from betraying the shivering that had begun at the sound of his voice. Dear heaven, she thought, had he been awake all the time? Did he know of her silent examination?

"Okay, tell me what to look for," Luke asked, frowning as he fiddled with his wrist alarm.

Ruthlessly disciplining her thoughts, Delilah ticked off the symptoms of a ewe in labor. And then, with a mumbled, "If anything happens, come get me," she made her escape.

She didn't know how long she lay awake in bed, waiting for the shivering to stop and sleep to come, but when she woke again it was full daylight and she had that jarring guilty sense of having overslept. Her first thought was—*Luke!* Her second thought was that the sheep must be all right or he would have called her.

Nevertheless, she threw on her clothes and tied her shoes with shaking fingers and almost ran to the barn, without stopping for a bite of breakfast. At the door she stopped to collect herself, breathing deeply of the frosty air and exhaling puffs of vapor. Luke always got the best of her when she lost her temper. No matter what, she'd be cool, calm, confident. *She* was the one in charge here. He was just . . . the hired man!

The hired man was leaning on a stall gate midway down the center aisle. "Shh," he said when he saw her, and beckoned. "Come here."

Delilah went to join him. All her good resolutions bolted, leaving her quivering with fury.

Curled up in a far corner of the stall were two big, beautiful, healthy lambs, sound asleep. Their mother had her head in a bucket near Luke's feet and was slurping with noisy gusto. Delilah recognized her immediately—it was old Blossom, one of the Hampshire cross-breeds that had been part of her very first flock. She was a bottle-fed pet, a sweet, stupid, gentle old thing, and a reliable mother.

"You didn't call me," Delilah stated carefully, getting a grip on her anger.

"Didn't see any need to," Luke said easily, reaching through the gate to scratch the woolly tuft on Blossom's forehead. "This old gal didn't need either one of us, did you, sweetheart?"

Delilah stared at him, speechless. His expression, like his voice, was possessively affectionate, almost besotted. She felt a creeping new emotion. Could it possibly be . . . jealousy?

"She'd already had one lamb when I got up at three," he went on. "Seemed to be doing fine, so I just watched and waited. The second one came along about fifteen minutes later. No problems at all."

Delilah "Humph'd" noncommittally and opened the gate. She knelt first to check Blossom's milk supply, then moved to the sleeping lambs.

"They've both nursed," Luke informed her with a proprietary air. "And I've already put iodine on their umbilical cords."

"And did you happen to notice—" Delilah began caustically.

"One of each. The female was first, but I think the male's a little bigger."

After a moment Delilah dusted off her hands and stood up without disturbing the dozing babies.

"I gave her some hay and water," Luke added, still fondly rubbing Blossom's grizzled head. "She sure was thirsty."

"They always are, after lambing," Delilah mumbled. He had, unerringly, done exactly the right thing. After clearing her throat she managed to add grudgingly, "Thanks." With her face averted she tried to slip past him through the gate.

His hand on the nape of her neck intercepted her. " 'Lilah . . ."

Her breath had backed up into her chest, putting a funny little catch in her sigh of vexation. "I knew it," she muttered. "I knew this was going to happen."

"Knew what?" he asked, turning her.

"You can't take orders," she said between her teeth, lifting resentful eyes to his face. "I told you to *call* me. I should have been here, dammit."

His gaze locked with hers and darkened. His mouth tightened, then relaxed. "If I don't take orders very well it's because I happen to have a brain, too, not to mention a certain amount of common sense. What's the point of having help if you're going to get up yourself for every ewe that lambs anyway? 'Lilah, it was routine. Even *I* could see you weren't needed."

While she stared at him in stubborn silence she was wondering why she was quarreling with him. She knew he was right. But her brain was mush! His fingers were stroking, massaging through the hair at the base of her skull. . . .

He gave a short, exasperated sigh. Delilah saw a muscle work rhythmically at the hinge of his jaw as his hands touched the sides of her neck, her shoulders, her arms. " 'Lilah," he whispered, "why are you making this so *difficult?*"

"I just . . . wanted to be here," she said faintly, knowing he wasn't talking about the lambing incident. "Can't you understand that?"

He was frowning, rubbing the sleeves of her sweat shirt up and down with his palms. He had a disconcerting habit of doing that, she thought, as if he were considering tearing away the fabric to get to what was underneath. She found herself hanging on to his arms to keep herself from falling into the wells of his eyes.

After a moment he said softly, "Yes, I think I do understand. You've been going it alone so long you don't know how to let go. Look, you have to learn that if you hire a man to do a job, you stand aside and let him do it."

She opened her mouth, then closed it again and gave

her head a little shake. Luke pulled her gently toward him, testing her resistance. His soft expulsion of breath was a punctuation mark of frustration. " 'Lilah . . . why do you keep fighting me? Why are you afraid of me?"

In a voice she didn't recognize Delilah heard herself answer, "I don't know."

It was an admission. She heard him acknowledge it with a tiny, involuntary sibilance. "Don't you know I'd never hurt you?"

His eyes had never been so compelling, his mouth so sensuous and—could it be?—vulnerable. And she'd never felt so muddled. "It isn't that." Her words were slurred, as if she were drunk. She frowned, knowing that, like someone inebriated, she was about to say too much. "I think . . . I'm afraid of losing control. . . ."

His laughter was gentle irony, not humor. "Would losing control be such a terrible thing?" Somehow his hands had slipped to her ribs, and now, though it was the cotton of her sweat shirt that he manipulated, it was the cool kiss of silk that caressed her skin. He tilted his head, smiling as he felt and analyzed that intriguing duality. "It might be . . . I think it would be a wonderful experience for both of us to lose control."

Through cotton, through silk, the warmth of his hands burned the sides of her breasts as he pulled her to him by slow, inexorable degrees. When her breasts brushed his chest, her stomach knotted and her nipples hardened painfully inside the restriction of her camisole. With a sharp edge of panic in her voice she cried, "That's not what I meant! I meant control of . . . what's mine."

"Ah, 'Lilah." His hands were slowly roaming over her back, holding her close, making her feel his body with all the length and breadth of hers. "You just can't help fighting me, can you?"

No, she couldn't. She shouldn't give in. But she had a feeling she was about to. Was this, she wondered, what it felt like to drown? Was there a moment, finally, when you grew so weary of the struggle that it felt good, so good, to give it up? Almost . . . like coming home.

" 'Lilah," he whispered, placing a kiss like a precious gift on the top of her head, "I don't want anything that belongs to you."

She lifted her face, searching his eyes. *Drowning* . . .

"I just want *you*."

Her eyelids dropped, and she felt the warm, moist brush of his lips on each one. *Drowning* . . .

"Just you . . ."

Her head fell back into the cradle of his hands. Her lips parted, and his breath merged with hers. With a sigh she let herself be immersed in his deep, drugging kiss. Her mind shut down and feelings took charge. Without anybody telling them to, her hands roamed where they pleased, learning and savoring new shapes and textures, and then moving on, hungry for more. . . . Raspy morning beard on hard male jaws; warm, taut neck, pulsing with life; round, palm-fitting shapes of shoulders and biceps; fabric; harsh and alien. She understood, now, the urge that made *him* want to cast that restriction aside. Warmth and wanting poured over her, a gentle inundation. . . .

Reality abruptly intruded, like the sudden, painful rush of cold, life-restoring air to her lungs. Her conscious mind broke free and struggled to the surface. Her instinct for self-preservation was stronger than the desire to surrender. She broke from him, gasping, "It's morning!"

"I know," Luke said softly. "We're not strangers anymore."

Delilah understood the reference to that strange first-morning kiss. *Love in the morning* . . . In near-panic she put her hands flat on his chest and pushed back against the circle of his arms.

"I just got up," she said, knowing she was babbling like an idiot in her desperation. "We haven't eaten breakfast yet. I have chores—"

They both froze, muscles tensed and gazes locked. Above their harsh and rapid breathing they could hear the distinct and unmistakable sound of a hoof rhythmically scraping concrete. Another ewe was in labor.

* * *

" 'Lilah . . . 'Lilah . . . Wake up, Blue Eyes. I need you."

Delilah clawed her way upward toward wakefulness, fighting a desire for sleep that clutched at her like sea-weed.

" *'Lilah.* Come on, babe, I think we've got trouble."

She put out a hand and touched the cold flesh of Luke's face. Without thinking, she hooked both hands around his neck and pulled herself out of unconsciousness and into the warm haven of his arms.

As his arms tightened around her he gave a funny, surprised little chuckle. "Come on, darlin'," he said firmly. "Wake up." He gave her a swift, hard hug and put her gently from him.

Delilah rubbed her eyes and muttered, "Wha' time is it?"

"Just past two. Sorry to wake you, but we've got two going at once, and I think that two-year-old you were worried about is in trouble."

"Okay," she murmured. "Be right there."

Luke nodded and left her to pull on her clothes and gather her sleep-starved wits. Thanks to him, she was averaging around five hours sleep a night—though she suspected he got by on considerably less. She knew there were times when he'd sat up alone with a laboring ewe—just to make sure—when he'd assured her he'd slept through a routine delivery. And, she acknowledged as she picked up her flashlight and stepped into the cold, the strain was beginning to show. Though his smile was as devastating as ever, she'd noticed that his eyes had developed shadows and his face a certain gauntness. She had an idea that in spite of the way he put away food, he'd lost weight. He hadn't had a single break since lambing started. Yesterday, during a lull that promised to be the calm before another storm, he'd insisted that she be the one to go into town for mail and groceries and a restorative lunch with Mara Jane, while he kept vigil over her flock.

How incredible, she thought. She'd grown to depend

on Luke MacGregor! Gradually, little by little, he'd become a part of her life. Now, after not much more than a week, she found it hard to recall a time when he hadn't been there. He was her rock . . . and yet there were times when she'd never felt more like an island.

Luke was a natural "toucher," but he touched the newborn lambs the same way he touched her. He was often gentle and solicitous toward her, even tender, yet he seemed to be holding himself apart from her. She found herself talking more than she usually did—or liked to—just to fill up *his* quietness, telling him things about her childhood, her father, herself, that she'd never told another soul. Luke was a good listener, and Delilah always reflected on their talks with the vaguely dissatisfied sense of having given away more than she'd received in return.

Luke rarely told her anything about himself. Except for a letter that had come for him the day before, bearing a Sacramento return address for Thermodyne, Inc., and its logo, he'd had no contact with anyone at all. And the letter hadn't been welcome. He had tightened his jaw and handled the letter almost warily, finally tucking it unopened into the inside pocket of his flight jacket.

When she thought back to her malicious little fantasy about the *Gentlemen's Quarterly* model up to his elbows, et cetera, she felt small and ashamed. Now, whenever she watched him down on his knees in the wet straw, helping a new baby learn how to nurse, his bare torso gilded with sweat and still showing the imprint of his straw sleeping pallet, something alien and frightening bumped against her ribs, clutched at her throat, and stung and smarted behind her eyes.

At those times she thought, *Dear heaven, it's really happening. I'm falling in love with him. . . .*

Luke looked up when Delilah came into the barn, damping down, as had become his habit, all physical response to her presence. It had become almost a natural reflex, like blinking.

"What's she doing?" Delilah asked. Her voice was still gravelly with sleep.

"Nothing," he told her grimly. "Absolutely nothing. Water broke maybe forty-five minutes ago, and since then she's done nothing but act miserable."

"And the other? Which is it?"

"The short one with the white face."

"Oh, the old Dorset?" She flashed him a ghost of a smile. "That's another of my pets, you know. Her name's Daisy Mae. She'll probably have white lambs. What's she doing now?"

"Very little, but I don't think she's in as much trouble as this one."

"Okay, let's take a look," Delilah said, opening the stall gate.

"Legs are folded back," she said tersely a few minutes later. "And it's a big lamb. Too big."

Luke said nothing, watching her impassively and marveling, as he always did, at the strength in those childlike hands and slender arms, at the fierce determination in the set of that soft mouth and delicate chin. And he thought, She's incredible . . . and so incredibly lovely.

Sometimes, though, strength and determination, no matter how fierce, aren't enough.

Luke finally had to look away from the small figure kneeling in the straw, desperately trying to save the lamb's life. It hurt too much to go on looking at her. He felt her pain like an ulcer in his belly—a steady burning that wouldn't leave him alone. Finally, still without looking at her, he put a hand on her shoulder and said huskily, " 'Lilah . . . Come on, give it up."

She shook his hand away and growled furiously, "*No! No* . . ."

After a few seconds, though, her frantic movements slowed, then stopped. She gave the still, lifeless form at her knees a poignant little pat and slumped back, exhausted and defeated.

"It was too big," she said in a tiny, drowned voice. "Too big for a first lamb. Why did she have to have a single? Why, damn it? I couldn't . . . I couldn't—"

"Of course you couldn't," Luke said harshly, unable to take any more. "You're not God!"

She winced as if he'd struck her, then jerked her head around to pierce him with a stare of bitter resentment. Her nose was red and her mouth swollen and trembling, and tears made glistening trails on her cheeks.

It occurred to him, not for the first time, that the only times he'd ever seen her cry had been for her sheep.

"You're not . . .God," he repeated softly, lifting his hands in a helpless gesture that betrayed his frustration at being unable to ease her anguish. "You can't save them all."

She shrugged with bravado, and said, "Oh, I know, I—" She broke off, squeezing her eyes shut in a futile attempt to stem a new flood of tears.

Luke watched the struggle in his own private agony, wanting to take her in his arms and comfort her, and knowing he couldn't allow himself to do that. After the last time he'd held her, he'd known that if he ever held her again he'd have to make love to her. He'd known that he *could* make love to her—she was his for the taking. It was what he'd worked for, what he was here for. And he'd also known that if he hurt this woman he'd never be able to live with himself again.

Sheep are wonderfully resilient. After an hour's rest the exhausted two-year-old ewe was up munching hay and searching the straw in a sporadic, absentminded way for the lamb her foggy instincts kept telling her ought to be there somewhere. By morning she would have forgotten even that.

Across the aisle from the two-year-old, the gentle Dorset was busy trying to mother her new triplets—tiny cuties with fuzzy white mutton-chop whiskers. Delilah knew the old ewe would never be able to feed all three lambs, and that, as welcome as the triplets were, it was going to mean another bottle baby to worry about.

The orchard door opened and Luke came in, blowing on his hands. He'd disappeared a short while ago without saying anything, but Delilah had heard the rhythmic scrape-thump of a shovel coming from the orchard and guessed he'd gone to prepare a resting place for the stillborn lamb.

"You didn't have to do that," she said as he came toward her.

"I know." He stopped beside the gate to the Dorset's stall. "Cute little devils," he said after a moment. "Can a ewe feed three?"

Delilah shrugged. "Some can. I don't think she can, though. She's too old."

Luke gestured toward the stall at Delilah's elbow and said, "Doesn't seem fair, does it? Can't you give one to her?"

"I tried," Delilah said tiredly. "While you were outside. She won't accept it."

"Won't accept it? How can she tell the difference?"

"Smell, probably. Somehow or other, after the lambs are born, while the mother is cleaning them, she 'imprints' her own lambs. And if she doesn't get to do that, she won't claim them or allow them to nurse. Period."

"Hmm," Luke said, crossing the aisle to join her at the two-year-old's stall. "So if she doesn't actually clean a lamb, she won't accept it. I wonder—did she ever try to mother her own lamb?"

"I know what you're driving at," Delilah said, rubbing her eyes. "I don't know. I guess she might have. We . . . left it in the stall when we were working with the Dorset, so it's possible. You're thinking of 'grafting' one of the triplets, aren't you? Using the skin . . ."

Luke lifted one shoulder, treading cautiously. "Ever tried it? Would it work?"

"I've heard of cases where it has," she said slowly, and swallowed hard. "I've never done it. I've just never—" She stopped, and Luke put his hand on her shoulder.

" 'Lilah," he said softly. "Let's try it. What've we got to lose?"

"I—" she began, and swallowed again. Something big was stuck in her throat and wouldn't go down.

"Let me help. . . ."

Let me help. It was his solution to every problem. Every challenge she faced, every trouble, he had to be the one to fix things for her. The trouble was, it was becoming so easy to accept it. . . .

"Well, well," Luke said sometime later with an unmistakable air of pride. "Would you look at that?"

Beneath his overcoat of mottled gray lambskin, the Dorset triplet's little white tail quivered ecstatically as warm nourishment trickled down his throat and into his belly. The young Suffolk ewe nickered softly, then went on unconcernedly snuffling grain from a shallow pan while her adopted baby drank his fill.

"It worked," Luke said smugly.

Delilah glanced up at him, but couldn't see his face. It was backlit by the fluorescent light in the ceiling, a bright halo around his dark head. *My guardian angel . . .* She smiled wryly. "Don't you *ever* get tired of being right? *Oh!*"

She had risen too quickly, and discovered in the process that her legs had been replaced with blocks of wood. She clutched at the stall divider for support and got Luke's arm instead.

"You okay?" he asked in an oddly gruff voice.

"My feet are asleep," she muttered huskily. "Give me a minute."

"I've got a better idea," he said, and deftly scooped her up into his arms.

Delilah gave a breathless whoop of surprise, then lifted her arms, clasping her hands together at the back of his neck. "You have a solution for everything, don't you?" she said softly.

"I used to think so." His eyes stared broodingly back at her from inches away, and the muscle in his jaw jumped. He cleared his throat and asked abruptly, "How are your feet coming along?"

"Fine," she whispered. "You can put me down now. If you want to . . ."

There was silence, eerie and absolute. Though Delilah knew there must be stirrings all around them, it was as if they existed in a vacuum.

At the back of his neck her fingers, with minds of their own, slowly unclasped and crept over the collar of his jacket to play with the raw-silk coolness of hair. Something flared in his eyes, like coals coming to life with a breath of wind. Delilah's lips parted. They had minds of their own too. Slowly, hesitantly, she touched his face with the backs of her fingers.

Luke's arms tightened reflexively. He muttered something under his breath and lowered his head, claiming her mouth in an explosion of pent-up passion that shocked them both. For Delilah the shock was a lightning bolt of pure desire. It convulsed her body, arching it up and into his, and brought from deep in her throat a small whimpering sound of need.

This was no sensual, erotic preliminary or declaration of intent. It was an unconditional surrender to elements out of control. Delilah knew that—and discovered that she didn't care. Nothing mattered, nothing existed, there was no reality except Luke's mouth—moist heat and a building pressure and persistent, all-consuming rhythms. . . . She existed in the eye of a whirlwind, revolving slowly, weightlessly, carried away by something too powerful to understand and pointless to resist. Under the circumstances, all she could do was surrender. So she did—and discovered that it was what she'd wanted to do all along.

How many times had he kissed her? Four? Five? In how many different ways? He'd kissed her deeply before, intending to arouse, but never like this. And never before had she kissed him back without restraint, matching him passion for passion. They ignited each other . . . fed each other's flames . . . consumed each other. . . .

Delilah broke first, sobbing for breath. Her head fell back, and with a growl of masculine domination he claimed the vulnerable curve of her throat with his mouth. She felt herself revolving again, and weightless, but this time she knew she moved through time and space. When she felt the rough caress of blankets and straw under her back, reality returned, even if reason did not. She reached up to touch his mouth with her fingers and murmured drunkenly, "Luke . . . ?"

"Yes, love," he said thickly against her throat, trailing fire along her neck to her ear before lifting his head to look down at her. His hand was on her forehead, gently stroking. "What is it?"

"Luke . . ." She tried to focus on his face, then gave up and let her heavy eyelids fall. "Please," she whispered, breathing in sobs. "Please . . ."

For a long moment his body was motionless except for the heartbeat that drummed against the palm of her hand. One of his hands lay on her forehead, the other at the curve of her waist. He said hoarsely, " 'Lilah—" and then, muttering something she couldn't quite hear, raked his fingers through her hair and lifted her hard into his kiss. His hand at her waist slid under her, lifting and locking her close to his body, so that when he rolled onto his back she moved with him. He drove his tongue deep again, and yet again, then withdrew, leaving her gasping. But he stopped only long enough to lift her sweat shirt over her head and toss it aside.

Now she held his face between her hands and lowered her mouth to his. His lips parted, and she found herself exploring him, learning to go deep with her own tongue, responding to the growl that rumbled in his throat. His hands were free now to roam where they liked—upward under the camisole to stroke her ribs, the sides of her breasts, her back; down over the swell of her jeans-clad bottom. He made an impatient sound and brought his hands back to her waist, probing inside the restricting denim. She responded instantly, lifting her body away from him so he could reach her fastenings, and his. . . .

When they were naked and he rolled her back under

him, she tore her mouth from his and cried out his name, overwhelmed, suddenly, and frightened.

His voice came, tense and urgent. "Don't fight it, sweetheart. Stay with me. *Stay with me.*"

Ten

She opened her eyes and saw his face, his eyes smoldering with passion, his mouth curved with tenderness, his forehead creased with concern. She made a low sound, a calming sound, and said huskily, rapidly, "It's . . . okay. I'm okay. I just—"

"I know." His lips brushed her forehead, then her lips, and she felt the heat of his slowly released breath. "I think . . . I'd better try . . . to slow things down." She heard the vibrance of restraint in his voice and felt it quiver through his muscles. He brushed her mouth again, and this time she tilted her head, nudging him with her lips. His tongue bathed her mouth with moisture, warm and sweet. She gave a hungry little chuckle and closed her eyes.

"Not *too* slow," she murmured against his mouth, adjusting her legs to make a place for him. He gave an answering laugh and sank into her kiss, resting his body for a tender, tremulous moment in the cradle of hers. The kiss became rhythmic, slow and hypnotic as jungle drums. Her body began to swell and ache and burn with a strange and compelling restlessness. She moaned and stirred, searching . . . until the muscles beneath her hands tensed and tightened, and Luke bowed his back, bringing himself into her at last.

She felt one small spasm of shock, and tore her mouth free to release a long, shuddering sigh. She'd never known such a sense of . . . completion, as if, for the first time in her life, she was all in one piece.

It was impossible for either of them to maintain the slower pace. After those few tender and critical moments, precious though they were, they didn't even want to try. Luke tried to hold back until he was sure of her fulfillment, but he knew it was a lost cause. The storm gathered quickly, and burst over him with a violence that left him drained and shaken. But as the mists of passion slowly cleared, he was delighted and humbled to feel *her* body swell and throb, and to hear her small cry of release.

As he held Delilah's trembling body, stroked and petted and whispered soothing phrases of endearment, he was thinking how lucky he was that it had turned out so well—no thanks, he told himself with some chagrin, to any particular skill or finesse on *his* part!

The small hand on his chest curled, and fingers burrowed through his hair to stroke his skin. He caught her hand and squeezed it, and planted a fervent kiss on the top of her head.

"Was that—" She stopped, then managed to ask in a very small voice, "Was that . . . what I think it was?"

Luke was stunned to silence. Dear Lord, he thought, could that possibly have been her first? He was fairly sure she hadn't been a virgin, but a first nevertheless?

Next time, he vowed silently, hugging her to him with a fierceness that made his chest hurt and his eyes sting. Next time . . .

Luke clawed his way out of unconsciousness, fighting through layers of thick, suffocating sleep. For days now he'd been running on sexual tension alone, and last night it had finally caught up with him, in more ways than one. He couldn't remember a time in all his life, including college finals and round-the-clock shifts on the oil rigs, when he'd felt so *tired*. He'd always been an early riser, but right now he'd have given a lot for an extra couple of hours of sleep.

It was pride that finally got him up. The baaing of hungry sheep and the clank of grain buckets colored his semidreams with visions of a small, dark-haired woman struggling to carry a heavy load of hay, all alone. He groaned and hauled himself into a more-or-less vertical position, railing at the morning. Sheer macho pride, he thought.

He pulled on the first things he could find—his flight jacket and the jeans he'd discarded in such haste last night—and stumbled to the door. The sun was bright, the frost had long since melted, and Delilah was coming toward him through the sheep-run, carrying the empty buckets. The instant he saw her he knew it wasn't only pride that had dragged him out half-asleep into the sunshine. He was hungry. And for once, it wasn't for food. He was hungry for the sight, the feel, the taste of Delilah. He'd thought last night had been the culmination of something. Now he knew it had only been the beginning.

Something was pricking him inside his jacket. Experiencing a sensation in his midsection similar to what happens when the elevator you're riding in suddenly drops thirty floors, he reached to the inside pocket to finger Pete's letter. It was pricking, all right—pricking his conscience. He hadn't opened it yet, but he knew what it said. *Mac, where are you, buddy? Why haven't you called? How are you making out with the Beaumont chick, man? We're running out of time. . . .*

But it had been a long time since Luke had thought of her as Judge Beaumont's daughter. Now she was just 'Lilah, and time had a new meaning.

She halted a few feet away and gave him a fierce, smoky look. "You look terrible," she said finally, sounding surprised.

He snorted ruefully and raked his fingers through his hair. "Things are lookin' up. Thank heavens I'm not 'beautiful' anymore!" After long, silent moments, he added very softly, "I'm sorry, but I can't say the same for you." He spread his hands and lifted his shoulders. "You look . . . incredible."

She colored, looked away across the orchard, then down at the buckets in her hands.

" 'Lilah," Luke said, his voice tense and husky, "if I move away from this wall it'll fall down. So for Pete's sake, *come here.*"

He saw her throat move. She put the buckets down with a funny, vexed little sigh and walked into his arms. For a while he just held her, resting his cheek on the top of her head. Her hair was silky-warm and smelled of hay and sunshine. She breathed another sigh—a relaxing sigh, this time—and murmured, "I was afraid that . . . I didn't want you to think—"

" 'Lilah," he said, hugging her fiercely, "*hush.* The trouble with you is, you think too much."

"Do I? I guess I must. Mara Jane said I should listen to my feelings, but I didn't—"

"*And* talk too much!"

Without another word she turned her face into the hollow of his neck and raised herself a little on tiptoe in order to kiss the underside of his jaw.

"Atta girl," he said with gravel in his voice. "You're getting the idea. But be careful. I'll scratch you."

She drew back and smiled up at him, laying a hand along his jaw to gauge the stubble. "You really are a wreck," she said with a happy giggle. "I didn't think it was possible."

"I can never figure out whether you're complimenting me or insulting me," Luke said plaintively, rubbing his face. "You have kind of a turned-around attitude about physical appearances."

"I think I *am* getting used to you," she said, studying him thoughtfully.

"*Used* to me!"

"Yes. Mara Jane said I would."

"I think I've gotta meet this woman."

"You will. But not," she said, horrified, "looking like *this.* You'll make a liar out of me."

"What?"

"I've already told her you look like one of her heroes. She writes romances, you know."

"Oh, Lord." They were both laughing, Delilah with her forehead pressed to his chest, Luke with his chin on the top of her head. "Oh, 'Lilah," he said, taking a breath, "how I l—"

He stopped, shocked by what he'd almost said. Something he'd never said before in his life. What shocked him the most was how *easy* it had been—as natural and right as drawing a breath.

Delilah knew she was in trouble when she found herself rummaging frantically through her kitchen drawers in search of candles. Not just candles—she had plenty of the stubby, burned-down variety she used during power failures—but tall, *new* candles, preferably white, still wrapped in cellophane, scented with something exotic and romantic . . .

She was in despair because the yellow oilcloth was too stark, the brown stoneware dishes too serviceable. And because she had no flowers, not so much as a sprig of sage.

And then she thought, Soft music and candlelight? Delilah, who are you trying to kid? He'll die laughing!

It was all too obvious. Even fixing supper was too obvious, for her. Games. It was all a matter of those seventh-grade games she'd hated so much, trying to be something she wasn't, just to please a man. And yet . . .

She did want to please him. She felt weak and shaky inside at the thought of him. She wanted him to know how she felt. But at the same time she was afraid to, because she wasn't really sure how *he* felt.

Oh, Lord, she thought, she just didn't know how to play this game. How did a woman go about telling a man she'd had a change of heart? How did she invite a man into her house—and her bed—without risking making a fool of herself?

In the end, Delilah didn't use the table at all. She put her brightest and best Navaho rug—a "storm" pattern, with touches of yellow highlighting the traditional red, gray, black, and white—on the floor in front of the sofa. Arranged picnic-style like that, she thought the old crockery didn't look half bad.

When Luke came in with the milk bucket she was on her knees trying to arrange some sprigs of dried buckwheat and wild oats in a pottery jug. She looked up and thought, Oh, help. She couldn't get up. What now? Her legs felt as fragile and brittle as the dried grasses in her hands. She managed a breathless and wary "Hi," then went on looking at him and rubbing her hands on her thighs. She focused on his eyes, afraid to see the expression on his face. After an endless moment's silence she waved a hand, then jammed both hands into her back pockets.

"Supper's almost ready," she said with defensive belligerence. "I hope you're hungry."

Luke's gaze swept over the carefully laid rug, the yellow cloth napkins, the dry arrangement in its earthenware jug, the earthenware bowl full of salad, the platter of cold fried chicken, and his mouth crinkled into one of his heart-stopping smiles. "Starved," he said without missing a beat, and carried the buckets to the kitchen sink. "What smells so good?" he asked casually as he poured milk into the waiting strainer.

Delilah took a deep breath. "Blueberry muffins," she said, hunching her shoulders protectively around her painfully thumping heart. If he said one word . . .

He said two, lifting his eyebrows at her over his shoulder. "No kidding?"

"Well," she hedged gruffly, "they're from a mix."

" 'Lilah," he said, setting the buckets on the floor and straightening, "when you said you'd fix supper tonight I was prepared for oatmeal and peanut butter. Blueberry muffins sound fantastic." His grin was the impish one, gently teasing and as contagious as laughter.

Under the buoyant influence of that grin Delilah felt light enough to rise to her feet, but the soft touch of his fingers on the top of her head forestalled her.

"Stay put, love. I'll get them," he said softly. "Anything else?"

"Just the milk," she said, then cleared her throat and settled back onto her heels. She watched him wash his hands, transfer hot muffins from the pan to a plate, take the pitcher of milk from the refrigerator, and settle onto the rug as if they ate every meal on the floor. The sight filled her with a fluttery, tremulous kind of wonder.

He was making it so easy, she thought. After all her worrying . . . Everything he did, he did with grace, without awkward places and bumps. Didn't he ever stumble? Didn't he ever feel uncertain?

"Nice rug," he commented. "One of yours?"

"What? Oh . . ." She had to shake herself. She'd been mesmerized by his hands as they selected a muffin, slowly broke it apart, and buttered it. "Yes," she murmured. "Mine." One of his hands, holding half of a still-steaming muffin, was extended toward her mouth. With a funny little catch to her breathing she parted her lips and snapped her gaze to his face. She watched him bite into the other half of the muffin and lick crumbs from his lips, and felt her tongue move in unconscious imitation of his. With a faint sigh she closed her eyes and opened her mouth to accept his offering. She chewed and swallowed, tasting nothing. Her throat had closed up tight. A whole troop of butterflies was holding a private party in her stomach.

His hand came toward her again, and his thumb brushed across her lips. "Crumbs," he explained softly, and, without taking his fingers from her lips, leaned across to touch her mouth with his. "Seems a pity to waste them . . ."

"Oh," Delilah breathed, and held very still. She waited until he had pulled away a little, then asked, "Why . . . didn't you do that before?"

"Before what?" The backs of his fingers were stroking her throat, making her want to swallow. The wooing resonances in his voice covered a shimmering spectrum of sound. If rainbows made noises, she knew they'd sound like his voice.

"Before now. Today. After . . . I was afraid," she muttered reluctantly, her throat muscles rigid with unexplained tensions, "that you didn't want to."

"Oh, 'Lilah," he said, smiling. "I didn't all day because I wanted to . . . too much."

"Did you?" She struggled briefly with the logic, then sighed. "I don't think I understand."

"Things happen when I kiss you, did you notice? Like last night. And I didn't want that to happen today."

"Oh," she murmured, beginning to pull away. "I see."

"No, you don't." He held her head in his hands, tilting it, forcing her to look up into those lethal, black-fringed eyes. The dissonances in his voice intensified, abrading her nerves, chafing her emotions. "I've wanted you all day. I woke up wanting you. Last night we got hit by lightning. Today . . . Today I want to love you slowly, completely. And there hasn't been time. So I couldn't let myself kiss you, because I wasn't sure I could stop at that. Understand?"

"Yes." She closed her eyes. "And now?"

"Now," Luke replied huskily, "we have time."

"What about dinner? You said you were starving."

"There're all kinds of hunger," he growled, and brought his mouth to hers, letting her feel the depths of his need.

Things happen when I kiss you, she repeated to herself. Things like heat and pressure and upheaval, deep, deep inside. Things that made her lose all sense of time and direction. Confusing feelings, like pleasure that made her want to cry, and aches that filled her up with joy.

These were the feelings Mara Jane had told her about! And she was right. The feelings were right. But . . .

"Luke!" she cried out in sudden panic, pulling away.

"What, love?" His voice and eyes were tender, and his fingers were like a whisper on the back of her neck.

"What's going to happen to us?"

"Don't you know? Whatever we make happen . . ." His mouth was a soothing, gentle warmth on her throat, his hands sure and steady on the buttons of her shirt. She moaned and let her head fall back in temporary surrender. His tongue stroked the hollow at the base of her throat as his hands pushed the shirt over her shoulders.

"Do you have any idea," he asked unsteadily, "how sexy it is, knowing, all day long, what you're wearing under this stuff?"

"No," she moaned, then shook her head and grasped at his wrists. "No. I mean, some things you don't *make* happen. They just happen. And it isn't right to just ignore everything and be carried along—"

"For Pete's sake, 'Lilah," Luke said with a kind of desperation, "what are you arguing about now?"

"I'm not arguing! I'm just . . ." She closed her eyes.

"What, dammit?"

"Well, what about the girl? The one you're hiding from—the one who wants to marry you. Remember her?" It cost her a lot to say it, and when she had finished she was trembling. Luke hesitated, then released her hands and sat back against the base of the couch. Delilah pressed her clasped hands to her mouth and waited.

There was a very peculiar expression on Luke's face. It was the first time she'd ever seen him look unsure of himself. He mumbled, "Uh . . . I have to explain about that," and raked his fingers through his hair.

Here it comes, thought Delilah. *He's already married.*

Luke regarded her warily, then laid his head back and looked exasperatedly at the ceiling. "The girl I'm hiding out from—Glenna. I have a confession to make. She's . . . um . . . my sister."

"What?" She stared at him without comprehension.

He shrugged and looked acutely guilty. "My sister," he repeated, and raised his arms in anticipation of Delilah's explosion.

She didn't disappoint him. "Your sister!" she breathed in an absolute fury. "You . . . jerk! You lied. You just plain out-and-out *lied*." She struck at his chest with her fist, then looked frantically at the supper for a more effective weapon. "And I, like a total fool, believed you! I can't believe I let you—"

"Whoa." Luke laughed, rescuing the jug of dried grasses and imprisoning her hands in his. "Don't break that. It's too pretty to waste on my head. Besides, you'd just have to sew me up all over again. Calm down, now. I didn't lie."

"What the hell would you call it?" Delilah shouted, unable to keep the quaver of rage out of her voice.

By contrast, Luke's voice was a patient, soothing murmur. "I did not lie. Every single word I said was the truth. Think back. I never said the girl wanted to marry me. I said she wants me to *get* married. And she does! Boy, does she ever. She's been after me for years. And now that she's gotten married herself, she's imp—"

"That's a crock, and you know it! You misled me! You deliberately made me think—" She was struggling against his grip on her wrists, trying to vent her anger and other more confusing emotions in a concrete way, but Luke suddenly laughed again and effortlessly pulled her across his lap and into his arms. Her breath caught. "You *are* devious," she whispered, looking up into his face. The anger was draining out of her, though, leaving her flushed and moist . . . and strangely weak and shaky.

"And you," he murmured, "are incredibly beautiful. And incredibly sexy. Especially when you're mad."

"I'm not mad," she said evenly, breathing hard. "And don't try to change the subject. What else have you lied to me about?"

For a long moment he looked down at her, with a gaze so dark and intense it frightened her. "Nothing," he said with a growl. "Absolutely nothing." And his mouth swooped down to take hers—a fierce possession, a declaration of masculine dominance, a territorial claiming . . .

For Delilah it *was* a lot like being struck by lightning. A jolt of pure desire stabbed through her, and she arched her body upward, hard into the curve of his. She moaned once, in futile protest and in surrender, and lifted her hand to touch his face.

His own hand raked down over her silk-and-lace camisole and slipped under it to whisper softly over the skin of her back.

"You lied to me too," he whispered into the moist heat of her mouth, pulling away a little.

She moved urgently, searching with her lips and tongue for more of the hot brandy sweetness of his mouth, and murmured an inarticulate denial.

"Oh, yes . . ." His hands explored her back from nape to waist, then moved across her ribs to the undersides of her breasts. "You *are* just as soft all over."

She held her breath as his thumbs traced the curve of her breasts and lightly circled the areolas. When the nipples hardened under his feathering strokes her eyelids drifted down and her lips softened into a smile. "I never said I wasn't," she whispered. "Just that I didn't use sheep's wool."

Luke chuckled and settled her more comfortably, supporting her body with one arm so that his other hand was free to roam at will. Delilah released her breath in a soft, uneven sigh and, lifting lids grown heavy with desire, gazed up into his face, his beautiful face. But what she saw wasn't perfect features and an angel's smile, or eyes that could melt glaciers. She saw a face with flaws. Stubble shadow on jaws and chin, tension creases around the mouth, smudges of purple under the eyes. A very human face . . . a beloved face. Luke's face.

She traced its lines and planes with her fingers the way a blind person "sees," as if with her sense of touch she could commit his face forever to her memory. As if she could imprint it, not just on her mind's eye, but on her soul's as well . . .

She saw his eyes close and felt a tremor run deep through his body. When her fingers touched his lips they parted, and grew vulnerable. Against her fingertips he whispered, " 'Lilah . . . I need you." Then his lips hardened, and with a quick, almost desperate movement he caught her fingers and drew them into his mouth.

Her laughter was a liquid sound more like a sob. In a husky whisper she said, "Make love to me, Luke," and in an instinctive gesture as old as womankind, she drew his head down to her breasts.

He easily slid the straps of her camisole over her shoulders. Her breast was a small, vibrant weight in his hand, its tip sweet and tender in his mouth. Moisture lay like gold dust on her skin. Her body arched and trembled beneath his hand, which traveled downward over her ribs and the taut hollow of her belly, over her jeans, to her drawn-up thighs. Her belly's concavity and the unyielding quality of denim provided him with a narrow access to her body's secrets. When he began to explore them with gentle fingers she moved restlessly against his hand and moaned.

"Easy, love . . ." he whispered. But he was the one who needed the advice, he thought. Her body was heated and swelling with passion, but the tension was in *him*. Her breath was coming in quickening gasps, but the deep-down inner trembling was *his*.

I need you. . . . Words he'd never spoken before. He'd said, "I want you" many times. But never "I need you."

To him, women's bodies were like fine and complex instruments. He understood and respected them, and had always prided himself on playing them with sensitivity as well as skill. But this, this was neither body nor instrument. This was . . . Delilah. And he was discovering, for the first time in his life, the difference between making love to a woman's body and loving a woman. All his acquired knowledge and virtuosity were worthless. Now he was functioning on instinct, and passion, and emotion, and for the life of him he couldn't seem to stop the trembling.

They stripped off the rest of their clothes. Her flesh was hot and fragrant, and tasted so sweet. He'd never felt such hunger, such a need to possess. She was his, just his, and he wanted—*needed*—to immerse himself completely in her, to bind her to him, body and soul.

His lips touched her belly and felt it quiver. His hands caressed her inner thighs and parted them, overcoming her slight resistance with gentle, loving pressure. His first touch was light—a kiss, tender and sweet. And then with slow, liquid stroking that deepened and deepened, he pleasured her, until he heard her cries and felt her body's inner throbbing in the depths of his own soul.

He held her and rocked her, murmuring words of comfort and praise. After a while he began slowly to arouse her again, and when he entered her he whispered with compelling urgency, " 'Lilah, sweetheart, open your eyes. *Look at me*. . . ."

And he held her eyes with his until for both of them the world dissolved into rainbow shimmers and sunbeams. . . .

About a week later Delilah stood at the door to her bathroom, staring at the transformed room. Luke had redone it. He had insulated it, put up drywall, tiled the floor, and put a radiant heater in the ceiling. And then he had installed a Victorian bathtub, claw feet and all.

It was the bathtub that had told her just how deeply and completely in love with Luke she really was, and how much she had already changed because of him.

She cried when she saw it.

"Do you know, that's the first time I've ever seen you cry over something besides your sheep?" Luke said as he held her.

"How did you know?" she asked him brokenly, lifting wondering eyes to his face.

"That you'd love a tub like that? Are you kidding? My little closet romantic?" He laughed and lifted her sweat shirt to fondle and caress her skin through a layer of silk and lace. " 'Lilah," he said as he kissed her, "anybody who wears what you wear and is as softhearted as you are has got to be a romantic at heart. And I can hardly wait to see you in that tub, up to your beautiful chin in bubbles. . . ."

Delilah shook her head and walked over to the table and sat down. Luke was in town, running an errand, and she was amazed at how lonely she felt. Lambing was almost over. What would she do when he left?

The sound of a car pulling up startled her, and she peered out the window to see Mara Jane climbing out of it.

Delilah met her at the door. "Mara Jane. What brings you up here?"

Mara Jane had a peculiar look on her face. "It's Luke," she said. "He . . . um . . . Roy just arrested him."

Eleven

"Luke, you . . . idiot," Delilah said softly, shaking her head and swallowing a persistent lump.

"Ouch—don't scold." He winced, and managed a lopsided grin. He was sitting on the corner of a cluttered desk in the small police station, his flight jacket across one knee and white gauze wrapped around his right hand.

Delilah took one step toward him. "You hurt your hand."

"Yeah." He lifted it slightly and shrugged. "I guess I cut it on old Amos's tooth. Should have aimed at a softer target."

"Luke, I can't believe you hit Amos Chappel! I thought you said that wasn't your style."

His mouth hardened, and he looked away briefly. "Yeah, well, sometimes . . . things happen to change your mind."

"What did he do, Luke?"

"Wasn't so much what he did," he mumbled, still not looking at her, "as what he said."

"My goodness, what did he say?" Delilah whispered, moving a step closer. Then she breathed a quick "Never mind!" when she saw the black anger in Luke's eyes.

"How bad is your hand?" she ventured, touching it gingerly with her fingers.

Luke gave a snort. "Not too bad." He tried another grin, and was more successful. "Won't need your needlework."

"You've bled all over your jacket again," she said, touching it. "Better let me take it . . . wash it out."

Luke suddenly swore and stood up, pulling her into his arms with restrained violence. After one startled gasp she relaxed against him, putting her arms around his waist and rubbing her face, kittenlike, in the open V of his shirt.

"Lord, I'm sorry," he said roughly into her hair. "Not that I hit him—the bastard deserved it—but I hate to put you through all this. Leaving you alone. 'Lilah, I think they're going to keep me here tonight. Roy's trying to get Amos to drop the charges, but—"

She drew back a little and looked up at him. "Hey. I'm used to being alone, remember?" Which may have been true once, but she had a feeling wasn't anymore. "Don't worry about me," she said staunchly, trying to reassure herself as much as him.

His eyes burned into hers. "I do," he said with a growl. "Can't help it."

"Oh, for Pete's sake," she said fiercely, moving her shoulders as if trying to shake off a burden. "I got along without you for two whole years, and after you go I'll . . . Dammit, I'll get along without you again. The lambing's almost finished anyway. I won't need you any—"

"Is that all you need me for? The lambing?" His voice was strained and tight. His face seemed dark, and etched with lines she'd never noticed before. Could this be the Luke MacGregor, the carefree charmer, who'd stepped out of a ruined airplane and into her arms, bloodied but unbowed? "*Dammit*, 'Lilah," he said, the hoarseness and passion in his voice ripping like a claymore through her defenses. "Forget about your damn sheep—your hired hand! What about me? What about *this*?"

His mouth swooped down and captured hers. His

hands held her head, fingers tunneling through her hair, rasping against her scalp. His mouth covered hers, and his tongue plunged deep and almost with desperation. . . .

A soft "ahem" interrupted them.

"Roy," Luke said thickly, tucking Delilah's head protectively under his chin. He held her tightly, stroking her hair, shielding her from embarrassment. "Any luck?"

" 'Fraid not." Roy's tone was dry. "He's still mad as hell . . . and who can blame him? I've seen prettier smiles on a jack-o'lantern. Nope"—he sighed with weariness and exasperation—"you're going to have to stay here tonight, buddy. Can't get your bail set till morning. Sorry."

"Yeah, yeah . . ." Luke took Delilah's arms and put her gently from him. "See that she gets home," he said, directing a black glare at Roy.

"I will," Mara Jane said softly, appearing beside Roy.

"Come on, Di," Roy said gently. "Mara'll take you home. Nothing you can do here till morning."

Delilah nodded, but didn't move, not quite able to tear herself away from the warmth and security of Luke's body.

" 'Lilah . . ." he said, his voice raspy. "I'll be fine."

Again she nodded, swallowing hard. "I'll take your jacket," she finally managed to say. "Get the stains out."

He nodded and handed it to her, letting his fingers linger on the inner bend of her elbow.

At least, Delilah thought as she followed Mara Jane into the cold desert nighttime, now she knew what it was going to be like when he left: Hell. Pure hell.

She had the jacket completely submerged in a sinkful of cold water before she noticed the letter in the inside pocket.

"Damn!" She swore aloud, snatching it out of the water, but not before it was well and thoroughly soaked. The ink hadn't run—it seemed to be waterproof—but she knew if she didn't spread the letter out to dry it would probably be ruined anyway. Overcoming an innate distaste for such an invasion of privacy, she carefully pulled the single sheet from its envelope and laid it face down on a dish towel, blotted it with another towel, and left it on the kitchen table to dry. With Luke's jacket soaking in the sink, she went out to check on the only three ewes left to lamb.

The night had never seemed so long, or so lonely. When Delilah went to the barn at one in the morning she found a two-year-old ewe in labor, and although she knew it was apt to be awhile before anything happened, she decided to wait. She hadn't been sleeping very well anyway. The vigil would have been a time of closeness and conversation if Luke had been there. Without him it was tedious and lonely. Last year she hadn't minded the boredom and the solitude, she mused.

But at least she had light now, thanks to Luke. She could pass the time reading the old newspapers she kept handy for wiping and drying the newborn lambs. (Newsprint was clean, absorbent, disposable, and, best of all, free.) Mara Jane had brought her a new batch only a few days ago—the *Los Angeles Times*, as well as local papers from both Bishop and Independence—so there was plenty to keep her occupied, if not especially interested.

One small item in the *Times*'s metro section did receive her undivided attention. The headline read: "Thermodyne Exec Escapes Injury In Plane Crash."

"Lucas Charles MacGregor," the article began, "president of Thermodyne, Inc., walked away uninjured after crashing his small private plane in a high Sierra meadow, a company spokesman announced Wednesday."

"Meadow, my foot," Delilah muttered. "And he was *so* injured. I should know!" She wondered just where the "company spokesman" had gotten his information. She began looking systematically through the local papers to see if they had anything more accurate to report.

She almost missed it. She was scanning headlines, keyed to the words *plane*, *crash*, and *Thermodyne*. She did a kind of delayed double take when she saw the headline, "Geothermal Hearing Set for April." And when she did, the name Andrew Beaumont jumped out at her with the insistence of neon. She read the entire article through twice and still couldn't understand why she felt cold all over, and especially down deep inside. . . .

All the time she was working with the two-year-old ewe, delivering a healthy set of twins, supervising their first attempts at nursing, she kept trying to make her mind focus on the article and what it meant. But her mind was numb. She couldn't make sense of anything. So Luke's company was under a federal restraining order—something to do with environmental impact and increased seismic activity in the Mammoth Lakes area. Big deal. So what?

So her father was the federal judge who had issued the restraining order that had shut down Luke's company. Small world. Extraordinary coincidence. Things happen like that all the time. It didn't have anything to do with *her*. She hadn't even *seen* her father in almost three years. Luke hadn't crashed his plane in her pasture on purpose, for goodness' sake! Had he?

But then, why did she still feel so cold?

Back in the house, she took off her coat and gloves and cap, but didn't go back to bed. There wasn't any point in it. She knew she wasn't going to do any more sleeping. Instead she paced, and pondered, pausing every so often to glance at the letter lying face down on a towel on the kitchen table.

She wouldn't read Luke's mail. She wouldn't. No matter how badly she wanted answers, she wouldn't stoop so low. . . .

The envelope was addressed, in a bold, masculine scrawl, to Luke MacGregor, care of Delilah Beaumont. Just a business letter—nothing unusual or mysterious about that. But why had he carried it around in his jacket pocket for nearly two weeks, unopened and unanswered?

She lost track of the number of times she picked the still-damp sheet of paper up and put it back down. And finally, feeling colder than ever and sick inside, she sat down at the table, pressed her knuckles against her mouth, pulled the limp page toward her with trembling fingers, and began to read.

It was midmorning by the time Luke got home. Feeling in critical need of a shower and shave, he went to the house first, even though he knew that at that hour Delilah would most likely be in the barn.

Something had crystallized in his soul during his night in jail, and it had nothing to do with the wisdom of nonviolence. His shocking reaction to Amos's sophomoric remarks about Delilah had knocked the blinders off, but it had taken the long, lonely night to make things absolutely clear. That was the last night he ever wanted to spend separated from Delilah, at least in the foreseeable future, and just possibly for the rest of his life.

He wasn't about to break that news to her, looking and smelling like a hard night on the town. He'd never in his life had a moment's uncertainty about a woman before, but with Delilah, the only thing he could be certain of was her unpredictability. He felt like a twelve-year-old trying to work up courage to ask the angel down the street to a junior-high dance. He needed the psychological armor of scrubbed hands and face and slicked-back hair, and a bouquet of hand-picked daisies.

When he saw Pete's letter lying on the kitchen table he felt as if someone had pulled his plug. The power that warmed and moved him was disconnected. He went still and cold. When he could move again he found that the cold hadn't left him, but had settled in his belly and in his heart, a blank gray fog.

It was too much to hope that she hadn't read it. From the letter's position it was obvious she had.

But, he thought, he hadn't read it himself yet. Maybe, just maybe, it was nothing. Maybe Pete hadn't said anything at all about the hearing, or Judge Beaumont, or Delilah, the judge's black-sheep daughter. . . .

"Mac, old buddy," the letter began, printed in bold

black, with the clumsy innocence of a child. Pete, the big, lovable jerk, had the brain of an electronic wizard and the heart of Huckleberry Finn.

"Everything around here is fine. What have you been up to? Must be going okay, or I guess I would've heard something, right? Just wanted to let you know, I talked to the lawyers, and Friedman thinks we have a good shot at getting Beaumont off the case. He says *any* 'close' relationship with Beaumont's daughter ought to be enough for a bias charge, so, good news: You don't have to marry the girl! It would be a good idea for you to call in once in a while, don't you think? When are you coming home? Sure could use a strategy session before the hearing. Call me!" (Double underlined.)

The letter concluded jovially, "Hang in there, Samson!" and was signed with the abstract squiggle that stood for "Pete."

"It *will* work," Delilah said levelly from behind him. She had come from the bedroom, he supposed. He turned and saw she was carrying his flight bag in her hand. "My father will almost certainly disqualify himself when he hears you've been living with me. Sleeping—"

"You read this? You opened and read my mail?"

"I wish I hadn't," she said in that same flat, emotionless voice. "I really wish I didn't have to feel guilty about finding out what a rat you are."

The pain hit him then, like slivers of ice that punctured every cell in his body. He hoped he'd stay frozen forever, because when the thaw came he knew he would disintegrate, like a frostbitten blossom. " 'Lilah," he began, but she shrugged her shoulders in a defensive gesture and set his flight bag on the couch beside his plastic suit carrier.

"It wasn't really necessary for you to go that far, you know," she said in a hard, tight voice. "My father is loaded with scruples. It was probably enough that you worked for me." She kept looking around the room as if searching for something, looking anywhere but at him. He watched her in silence, wanting to go to her and shake her, and then wrap her in his arms and make it right again, but knowing he couldn't. He had blown it, utterly and completely, broken beyond repair something precious and irreplaceable. He was overwhelmed, suddenly, by heartsick despair and a kind of shocked repudiation. *All the king's horses and all the king's men . . .*

If she'd been anybody but Delilah, he might have tried to explain. But she *was* Delilah, the proudest, most stubborn, bullheaded woman he'd ever met! Still, he made one effort. Feeling as if he were gargling metal filings, he protested, "I didn't even open the damn letter. Doesn't that tell you anything?"

She tilted her head thoughtfully. "You know, I wondered about that a little. It's just one of a lot of things I've wondered about, Luke, and you know what? I bet you'd have some dandy answers for all my questions. You're very good at coming up with plausible-sounding stories and explanations."

" 'Lilah . . ." he breathed on a long, anguished exhalation. But he had his pride too. He wouldn't plead and grovel, not for anyone! Damn it, he'd lived with the woman for three weeks! They'd shared so much, intimacies of body, mind, and soul. He'd given her the very best of himself—and she could so easily and so quickly believe the worst. All right, he'd blown it all to hell. He had no one but himself to blame. But how could she just forget everything that had been between them? *Everything . . .*

She took a deep, shivery breath and lifted a hand to forestall the denials he had no intention of making. He saw how shattered she was, and how unreliable the glue that held her together. He felt himself breaking up and flying apart, and knew that he wasn't ever going to be able to retrieve all the pieces.

"I'm not unreasonable," she said. "I'll give you until noon tomorrow to get yourself and your airplane off my land. That's more than twenty-four hours. In the meantime, if you have any decency in you at all, please don't let me see you, or hear your voice."

The moment stretched and finally splintered, and he nodded and reached for his flight bag.

"You know, what's funny," she said softly as he paused in the doorway, "is that it wasn't even necessary. My father would have given you a fair and unbiased hearing. Andrew Beaumont may be a lousy father, but he's a damn fine judge!"

She knew she was being unreasonable. There was no way it was going to be humanly possible for one man to get that airplane out of the pasture. He was going to need men and equipment, and that was going to take more than twenty-four hours, especially since he would have to go to town to call for help.

That didn't keep Luke from attacking the problem with a determination that bordered on obsession. As Delilah watched with grim fascination from the barn, he took the jack from the pickup and loaded the wheelbarrow with cement blocks left over from the construction of the barn. Could it really be just pride that was driving him, making him wrestle that wheelbarow up the hill through rough pasture stubble, arm and shoulder muscles straining and bulging, the tendons in his neck standing out like ropes? He had to be the most arrogant, stubborn, bullheaded man she'd ever met! Lord, how he hated to lose!

By midafternoon he had the plane on blocks, an arrangement that looked to Delilah to be precarious at best, because of the slope of the pasture. As she watched him from a distance, his tinkering and banging around the landing gear, she began to feel a creeping uneasiness. She'd hurled an ultimatum at Luke that she'd known very well he couldn't meet. He'd taken it as a personal challenge. What lengths would he go to, just to save his stupid macho pride?

At about three o'clock, he got into the pickup and went rocketing down the mountain in a cloud of dust. When he came back at chore time with an acetylene torch and an assortment of tools, Delilah's fears hardened into dreadful certainty. It was obvious that Luke intended to try to fly the airplane out of her pasture!

She flew through the evening chores on the crest of a wave of nervous energy that made her feel jangled and shaken. She didn't know what to do. She couldn't very well march up there and tell him to knock it off. She was the one who'd given him a deadline. If she backed down and released him from it . . . Well, she had her pride, too, dammit! But if he tried to take off from that rough little pasture, with patched-up landing gear . . . Suppose he was injured . . . or killed . . .

It was almost dusk. She carried the milk buckets to the house and then, in an emotional turmoil unlike anything she'd ever experienced, trudged up the hill to the pasture gate. She stood for a moment biting her lower lip and listening to the steady whoosh of the welding torch. Then, with shaking hands, she untwisted the wires that held the gate shut.

Luke was on his back under the plane, engrossed in his work. The blue welding flame flickered and darted across the reflecting safety shield that covered his face, making him seem more than ever like some strange, alien being. She waited for a moment, then swallowed hard, jammed her hands into the pockets of her windbreaker, and nudged his tennis shoe with her toe. He flipped up the visor of his shield and squinted at her.

"Don't look at the flame," was all he said, yelling above the roaring of the torch. "It'll damage your eyes."

She shifted her gaze angrily to his vulnerable midsection, and for some inexplicable reason felt herself fill up with tears. Rage, she told herself, fighting hard for control. She'd concentrate on the rage, the betrayal. She'd never let him know how he'd hurt her. Never.

"What do you think you're doing?" she shouted finally.

"What does it look like?" he shouted back without pausing in his work.

"You can't . . . you're not thinking of *flying* this thing out of here!"

He turned off the torch and lifted his visor. His eyes slammed into her like high-calliber bullets; then he shuttered them and shrugged. "Why not?" he said with a wry smile. "It's the only way I know of to get it out."

She threw her arms wide in an angry gesture of repudiation, and accidentally struck the wing with a resounding thump. The plane settled on its blocks with an ominous crunching sound. "You could . . . cut it up! Use that torch to cut off the wings and—and *drive* it out!"

"Over my dead body!"

"If you try to fly this thing out of here, it probably will be!"

"Do you care?" he asked bitterly, and she yelled violently, "No!"

He jerked himself upright. They stared at each other like angry children, breathing hard, eyes glittering, brimful of fire and water. And then, in the echoing silence, they both heard a grating noise.

Luke's eyes snapped upward to the plane's underbelly. He swore, and grabbed at the struts of the landing gear.

Delilah stood like a stone, frozen in an expression of horror and rejection of the situation, while inside her icy shell her scream echoed and reverberated: *"No! Luke!"*

But the plane's slow-motion slide was forward, downhill, onto its nose and directly toward Delilah. She heard Luke's shout above the nerve-shattering screech of metal on concrete—" 'Lilah! Move!"—but she couldn't seem to make anything work. She stared with incredulous eyes and wide-open mouth at the yellow monster bearing down upon her.

Something kicked her in the ankle, then hooked and yanked it out from under her. She fell backward, landing with a thud that drove the air from her lungs. With a noise like the dying scream of some huge prehistoric beast, the plane toppled slowly onto its nose.

Twelve

It probably should have crushed her head and chest like precious, fragile shells, Delilah thought later. But because Luke had knocked her backward it was only the propeller that caught her. It pinned her left leg to the ground like a twig broken under a sheep's hoof.

She didn't lose consciousness, though she seemed to be protected by some kind of shock. She knew something bad had happened, but it had an unreal quality about it, like a nightmare. There wasn't even very much pain. The worst of it was hearing Luke's agonized voice calling her, and not being able to answer him, to tell him she was all right. She opened her mouth and thought loving reassurances with all her might, but though she could feel the strain in her throat and chest, no sound came out. By the time he dropped to his knees on the grass beside her, she was on the edge of panic. She'd just discovered she couldn't breathe, either.

" 'Lilah," Luke said raggedly. "Thank God." His fingers briefly explored her face, her hair. He grasped her waist and gently lifted; lowered, then lifted again. Air screamed through her lungs.

"Easy, easy," he murmured soothingly, laying a calming hand on her forehead. "It's all right, love, don't panic. You had the wind knocked out of you. Okay now?

Feeling better?" His hand smoothed the hair back from her face, then slipped under her neck and gently lifted. His eyes swam above her, very dark, and creased around with concern.

"No," she said, testing her voice. It sounded strange to her—distant and tinny. "My leg is stuck. I think it's broken."

Luke carefully lowered her head to the ground. Vexed, she instantly raised herself on her elbows so she could see him as he knelt beside her legs. His back was toward her. "Luke?" she said. "How bad is it?" She saw him drop his hands to the ground and lean forward, supporting himself on them. He lowered his head and became very, very still.

Delilah shifted uneasily and croaked, "Luke, don't you dare pass out on me! I swear, if you leave me—"

He threw her one terrible look and left her. Before she even had time to worry about that, he had returned with the jack and was working in grim and feverish silence.

Mercifully, when the weight of the plane came off her leg, she fainted. When awareness returned, her leg was encased from the hip down with what looked and felt like an air mattress, and she was being lifted with infinite care, as if she were a newborn baby.

"Luke?" She put up a hand to touch his face and found it wet. Sweat, she thought fuzzily. It wasn't hot. Why was he sweating?

"Yes, love. I'm here."

"Don't go 'way," she muttered groggily. "Don' want you to leave . . ."

"I don't intend to." His words were muffled from the effort as he stood with her in his arms. She wasn't absolutely certain that he added, ". . . Ever again."

The trip down the mountain was an experience Delilah hoped to forget as soon as possible, but she knew it would probably remain etched in her memory for the rest of her life. She had to sit crossways on the front seat of the pickup, her back against the passenger door and her air-splinted leg cradled in Luke's lap. He drove as carefully as he could, but her pickup could be counted on to find and magnify every crack, pebble, and pothole in the road. Delilah thought of her ancestors and tried to be stoic.

They recited nursery rhymes, finally, to take her mind off the ordeal. It was Luke's idea, and Delilah was surprised to discover that he could remember a good many more than she could.

"How'd you know that?" she asked after he had finished a ditty about someone who stepped in a puddle up to his middle and never went to Gloucester again. Her head was resting against the cold window glass; she watched him from under eyelids too heavy to open more than halfway.

He glanced at her, as he did every few seconds, as if to assure himself she was still with him. "I don't know," he mumbled evasively. "Guess I must have picked 'em up from my sister. Hey—" He threw her a twisted grin. "Here's one I bet you know. 'Baa baa black sheep, have you any wool?' "

" 'Yes, sir, yes, sir, three bags full . . .' " Delilah sing-songed dutifully. She was thinking, though, that he looked awful. She must have scared him to death. Or maybe it was just that he couldn't stand seeing anyone in pain. Anyone at all . . .

There was a shadow made by a venetian blind on the wall. Delilah didn't have venetian blinds. "Where *am* I?" she muttered without much originality, frowning because it seemed very late, long past chore time, and she'd overslept again. She struggled to sit up and encountered resistance. Her left arm was strapped to something and connected by a tube to an upside-down bottle of clear liquid. The tube ended in a needle, which was inserted in the back of her hand and held firmly in place with a crisscross of white tape.

"What's this?" she asked of no one in particular, and was surprised to get a reply.

"That's an IV drip," a nurse informed her cheerfully, coming around from behind the bed. "Let's see . . . antibiotics and glucose—for infection and fluid replacement. My, you *have* had a time of it, haven't you, hon? Looks like you have a compound fracture. But you're going to be just fine."

"Fine," Delilah said hoarsely. She remembered it all now. How could she be just fine, when there were nearly three hundred sheep up on a mountainside depending on her for food and water? What in heaven's name was she going to do? If only Luke were here . . .

Luke. She remembered everything about him too. Pain knifed through her, eclipsing even the dull throbbing ache in her left leg. *Oh, Luke . . . Damn you! Where are you when I need you?*

"Your breakfast is here," the nurse said kindly. "Feel like you can eat something this morning?"

Delilah shrugged, and mumbled, "Sure." It was all she could trust herself to say. Tears seemed very close to the surface.

The nurse smiled at her and went out. Soon after, Delilah could hear some sort of commotion taking place outside in the hallway—low-voiced arguing, some scuffling sounds. The nurse came back in, looking flustered. "You have a visitor," she said, sounding affronted. "It isn't visiting hours, but he insists—"

"Luke?" Delilah's heart skittered wildly, and she lifted one hand to her hair in an automatic and purely feminine reaction. But the voice that was raised suddenly in indignation and authority was dry and precise, with none of the warmth and spine-tingling dissonances of Luke's.

"I have come," Andrew Beaumont announced, "to see my daughter. And I *mean* to see my daughter!"

"Daddy?" Delilah's voice emerged sounding thin and childish. She stared incredulously at the man who had just pushed his way past the stainless-steel breakfast trolley and into her room—a slightly-built man with a nut-brown, deeply lined face and shrewd blue eyes. She swallowed hard, and whispered, "Daddy." Her heart was pounding. Incredible, she thought. She was a grown woman, had been independent for years. How was he still able to intimidate her like this? "What are you doing here? How did you—"

"Luke MacGregor called me. Last night. Rather late, as a matter of fact."

"Luke . . ." Delilah's throat felt cramped and stiff. She cleared it futilely. "Is he . . . ?"

"He said to tell you he's gone home." Judge Beaumont passed the message on to her with characteristic precision. "And he also said to tell you not to worry about your sheep. He's taken care of everything."

"He would," she muttered. "He . . . um . . . he said exactly that? That he'd gone *home*?"

"Exactly." Her father eyed her keenly. "I take it that has some significance for you?"

"Yes," she said, staring miserably at the ceiling. "It does." So Luke had taken her at her word, she thought. She'd told him she never wanted to see him again, and it looked as if she never would. She wondered who he'd found to take care of her sheep. *Where is the boy who looks after the sheep? Under the haystack, fast asleep. . .*

"Um . . . would you . . . like to sit down?" she asked politely, indicating the one straight-backed chair in the tiny room.

The judge waved a hand, rejecting her offer. "I've been driving all night. I believe I'd rather stand." He folded his arms and regarded her with the critical, measuring stare she remembered so vividly. "You look very well, considering. I understand the sheep business is going well."

"It was," she said with a snort of painful laughter. "This accident pretty well tears it. By the time I pay someone to take care of things, the medical bills . . ."

Her father lifted his brows. "You're covered by insurance, if that helps."

"Insurance?" She frowned at him. "I'm not. I've never—"

"I've always kept you adequately covered," Andrew

said in his matter-of-fact way. "You've always been so headstrong, it was only a matter of time before you got yourself into trouble."

"You've covered me with medical insurance? *Why?* I'm twenty-six years old!"

"Why?" He looked taken back. "Well, because you're my daughter. I kept you on my policy all through college, and then later . . . I was quite certain you wouldn't have your own insurance, under the circumstances . . . Delilah, what is the matter?"

Delilah was laughing. Not with joy, or humor, but silently and painfully. "Oh, Lord," she breathed, covering her eyes with her unfettered hand. "And I thought I was so self-sufficient. So independent."

"I know. You've always tried to be. Even when you were a small child. It has . . . made you somewhat difficult at times, 'Lilah."

It was the first time he'd ever called her that. No one called her that . . . except Luke.

She slowly uncovered her eyes. Her father was standing with his back to her. His voice seemed strange, almost sad. After a moment he went on, as if delivering a presentencing lecture. "However, I trust someday you'll learn that no one is ever . . . completely independent."

"Funny," she said slowly, and her father turned to look at her, raising his brows interrogatively. "Someone else told me the same thing recently." No, she wasn't an island, and she wasn't independent. She never had been.

She shut her eyes tightly, but tears squeezed under her lids and trembled on her eyelashes. She heard her father stir restlessly and tried to laugh, knowing tears would scare him to death. But instead of laughter, her voice came out in a watery squeak. "Daddy . . ."

She felt him move to her bedside, hesitant and stiff. When he patted her hand she clutched his unashamedly, knowing it was probably all she was going to get from him. She was stunned when he leaned over, awkwardly, and kissed her forehead. She gave a startled gasp and held very still, hardly breathing, while an ache she had carried around with her for most of her life faded slowly away. She understood at last. He *did* love her. He'd never been able to tell her so, or demonstrate it with signs of affection, and he probably never would. But he loved her.

"Daddy," she said with a sniff, suddenly pulling away to stare at him, "you're wearing a *hat!*"

The judge took the floppy-brimmed blue thing off, looked fondly at it, fingered a few of the flies that decorated its crown, and jammed it back onto his head. And then, to Delilah's complete amazement, he grinned. "My fishing hat," he explained with a rather touching air of pride.

"Fishing!"

"My dear, you are obviously not aware that you are living in the middle of one of the richest trout fisheries in California!"

"No," she said faintly. "I guess I'm not." The idea of her father fishing, or enjoying *any* form of relaxation, was mind-boggling.

"There has been a recent development," Andrew said with satisfaction, giving his hat a pat, "which has cleared my calendar for a few days. I intend to get in some serious fishing." He tugged the sleeve of his jacket up and peered at his watch. "I'll be going. I've upset the nurses enough for one day, but I suspect I will be allowed to see you tomorrow at the proper time."

After her father left, Delilah had the strange experience of weeping copiously and smiling, even laughing a bit, at the same time. She'd never been such an emotional basket case. With all that was going on inside her, she barely noticed the ache of her broken leg.

How ironic, she thought, that she should finally rid herself of an old, old hurt, just in time to have it replaced with a new one. But it wasn't an even trade. The old hurt had been . . . familiar, dull, like a faithful companion that could be ignored a good deal of the time. The new one was raw and insistent—a vibrant, technicolor intruder.

Luke, you . . . rat, she cried silently and bitterly. *How could you do this to me? How could you make me love you, and need you so much, and then go off and leave me all alone?*

"Well. Don't we look nice this morning," said the nurse. She seemed oddly flustered. "I see we're all checked out and released. Aren't you happy to be going home?"

"Yeah," Delilah said dully. "Happy." Why not? Her leg was mending without complications, she'd been okayed for crutches and was learning to get around on them fairly well. Life was a bowl of cherries. Her father had stopped in to see her briefly every day before going off to try some new stream. Mara Jane and Roy had come and brought flowers. They all told her how fine everything was. There was nothing whatsoever for her to worry about except getting well. To Delilah they all seemed evasive and edgy, like lousy poker players with great hands.

"Well," the nurse said, beaming nervously, "I'm glad to see you're ready to go, because someone's here already to get you." She opened the door. "You can come in, sir. She's all ready."

Delilah was wryly amused to know that she wasn't the only one intimidated by the judge. But it wasn't her father who walked into the room. She stared in shock at the man, and after a moment the nurse cleared her throat and backed out the door. "I'll go . . . find a wheelchair," she muttered breathlessly, and fled.

No wonder she was nervous, Delilah thought. Her own stomach had climbed into her throat and was sitting on top of her voice box. She cleared her throat and swallowed in a vain effort to dislodge the lump. Dear Lord, she thought, he really was beautiful. . . .

At last she managed to say faintly, "Luke. What're you doing here?" He was wearing a sweater, some sort of light cable knit, and jeans. He needed a haircut—the thick, glossy chestnut hair was beginning to creep down the back of his neck. She decided she liked it that way.

He stood near the foot of the bed, tapping his fingers

restlessly on her bed tray and studying her with a narrowly focused black gaze. "What does it look like?" he said finally, sounding a bit surly. "I've come to take you home."

"I don't understand. I thought my father—"

"The judge has discovered a stock of native Sierra golden trout in your creek. He was kind enough to lend me his car."

"His car?" Delilah said with a squeak, utterly confused.

Luke smiled for the first time, the lopsided way. "Well, I could hardly take you home in the Hulk, could I?"

She shook her head, more to clear it of confusion than in agreement. "*My* creek? But I thought . . . Has he been staying at my place?"

"Yes," Luke said, watching her warily. "I gave the judge your bed. After one night on that couch of yours I moved back out to the barn. Of course," he added blandly, "we'll have to change the sleeping arrangements now that you're coming home."

"Home," Delilah echoed. "Then . . . you . . . *you've* been taking care of my sheep? Everything?"

"Well . . . the judge and I have, yeah."

She wondered if she could be having a nightmare. The idea of Andrew Beaumont tending sheep was so fantastic, it was disorienting, even a little frightening, like having normal, familiar objects turn into something weird and alien.

"Why didn't someone tell me?" she whispered. "I mean—my father, Mara Jane, Roy—they all knew, and they didn't tell me!"

"Well," Luke said with gravel in his voice, "they probably weren't sure how you'd take it. The last time we talked, you gave me twenty-four hours to get out of town, remember? You have a reputation for stubbornness."

"Stubborn? *Who's* stubborn! The last time I saw you, you were trying to fly a broken-down airplane out of a sheep pasture! Of all the stupid, nitwitted things to do! Almost killed us both!"

"Whoa. The fault for that accident is debatable. If you hadn't been so ready to jump to conclusions, fly off the handle—"

"Me! What other conclusion *could* I jump to? What are you hanging around for, anyway, guilt? You got what you wanted! Why in hell don't you just go!"

"You still don't get it, do you?" He was bending over her, one hand braced on either side of her pillow, his face dark and angry. "Talk about nitwits! You've had all this time to think about it and you still haven't figured it out!"

After a long tense pause of furious dagger-stares and rapid breathing, Luke closed his eyes and sighed. Then, as if in surrender, he ducked his head and kissed her. She gave a small, shocked whimper, and then, with a distraught moan, ran up her own white flag.

Her body felt hot and hollow. He poured himself into her—his passion, his frustration, his hunger—and she drank from him as if she would never get enough. She wasn't entirely sure what it all meant, but for now she decided she just didn't care. This was enough. He was here, and he was kissing her as if the world would end tomorrow.

Behind them the nurse coughed, and said brightly, "Well, here we are. All ready to go?"

Luke took his time, releasing Delilah's mouth by slow, reluctant degrees. Still holding her with the tractor beam of his eyes he murmured, "Yeah, we're ready. We're going *home*." He gathered Delilah up and, ignoring the nurse's dithering, lowered her carefully into the wheelchair and adjusted the support under her injured leg.

The nurse fussed helplessly. "Wait—sir—you can't—hospital regulations—"

Luke waved her away and took the handles of the chair firmly in his own hands.

It was an absurdly idyllic April day. The apple trees were in full bloom, bees were buzzing, the pasture was showing new green, and across its length and breadth a flock of charcoal-gray lambs gamboled and played, reveling in the spring sunshine. Delilah could almost hear background music—flutes, of course—playing the pastorale from the *William Tell* Overture.

She was sitting in the orchard, with her leg propped on a pile of sheepskins. Lady was asleep, her muzzle propped on Delilah's leg. Apple blossoms sifted lazily down all over everything, like snowflakes.

Delilah was preparing to warp her loom. She considered warping a loom the most exciting part of weaving. It was an almost mystical process—the birth, the conception, of a new project. It required a long, unbroken period of solitude—although she'd never had to worry about that before Luke had come into her life.

But Luke had promised her this day. He'd set up her large outdoor loom in the orchard, while he, with the part-time help of some local high-school "ag" students, took care of the sheep. The judge had left before breakfast this morning to make the long drive back to Sacramento, and Luke had sworn a solemn oath not to disturb her unless she needed him. He'd even hung a sheep bell on a branch within easy reach, so she could call him. Luke thought of everything.

Delilah sat with her supplies spread out around her and her hands idle in her lap, gazing through the frame of her loom at the frolicking lambs. It was one of her favorite sights. A good crop. A beautiful crop. She should be proud, and happy.

Instead she was depressed. It didn't feel like her place anymore. She felt . . . displaced, usurped, a guest in her own home. *Luke* was in charge.

She still wasn't exactly sure why he kept staying around. Guilt, probably. A sense of responsibility. Undoubtedly he felt at least partly to blame for her accident. She'd thought it didn't matter why. She loved him, and it was enough that he was here. Now it seemed she might have to choose between love and sanity. Luke was driving her crazy.

The front door slammed. Voices drifted up to her on

the soft air, coming unmistakably closer. Lady jumped up and went to investigate. Delilah looked around in exasperation. He'd *promised.*

He was coming through the orchard, his arm around a slender young woman with soft, honey-blond hair. As the woman turned to smile up at him, the breeze blew a strand of hair across her upper lip. Luke lifted his hand and carefully tucked the errant lock behind her ear. To Delilah, that gesture *was* Luke—solicitous, protective, possessive . . . smothering.

She knew who the visitor had to be, of course, and was already smiling a sincere welcome. Luke held out his arms in a gesture of abject apology and said, " 'Lilah, I know I promised, but Glenna has to go on to Tahoe, and—"

"It's all right," Delilah said, laughing. "This must be your sister. What a nice surprise!"

"You're not kidding," Luke said, beaming happily at them both.

"I hope you don't mind," Glenna said, "my just *coming* like this. I finally gave up hope of ever hearing from Luke, and decided to track him down. He's been avoiding me, I think."

"See?" Luke muttered in an aside to Delilah. "What did I tell you?"

Glenna gave Luke's waist a squeeze, forgiving him the private joke at her expense. "I'll bet he didn't tell you he was on his way to my wedding when he crashed, did he? He was *supposed* to give me away. Some people will do anything to avoid a wedding!" She punched him gently in the stomach. "I just had to come see for myself that he was okay, the rat. I really didn't expect to find *you* injured instead. I won't stay long, I promise."

"It's okay, really," Delilah said quickly. "I . . . decided I'm not really in the mood to do this today, anyway."

"Oh—you're going to start something! A rug? Or a saddle blanket? I've never seen the Navaho warping process before. I'd love to watch, if you'd let me. . . ." Glenna was wearing a crisp white linen skirt, and she carefully tucked it under her bottom as she squatted on her heels in the dirt beside Delilah.

Delilah stared at her. "Do you know weaving?"

"Oh . . ." Glenna made a gesture of self-deprecation. "I've had a class or two. But I love it. Someday I'd like to learn a lot more—how to dye my own yarns, spin, all that stuff. But Navaho weaving . . . that's . . . This is just fantastic. I saw some of the things you have in your house, but I never dreamed that *you*—Luke never told me!"

"I haven't had a chance," Luke pointed out mildly, "to tell you much of anything."

"Delilah," Glenna said earnestly, touching the rough frame of the loom with reverent fingertips, "do you have any idea what this is worth? I mean, there are people in my weaving classes who would have killed for a chance to learn real Navaho weaving techniques. And you have the fleeces and everything, right here. And of course the finished rugs—Good Lord, they're worth their weight in gold. Did you know that—"

"Whoa!" Luke interrupted, laughing. "Glenna's off and running. I see Josh is here to help me lay that water line to the barn. I'll leave you two to get acquainted while I get him started."

"Go, go," Glenna urged, shooing him away. "We will survive without you, although I realize that's hard for you to believe." As he grinned and walked away, she turned back to Delilah. "Seriously, Delilah, you could really turn this weaving of yours into money if you wanted to. I don't know how reliable the sheep business is, but if you ever needed extra cash . . ." She shrugged and stood up, brushing down her skirt and looking around her.

"I'll keep it in mind," Delilah said faintly, feeling slightly winded. Goodness, was the whole family like this? she wondered. Hell-bent on solving everyone's problems?

A little silence fell, the slight awkwardness of two strangers finding themselves suddenly alone. Glenna took a few steps toward the pasture, ducking her head under a low-hanging branch frothy with apple blossoms.

"It's really lovely here," she said, and after a moment added, "Is that where it happened, over in that field? Is that where Luke crashed?"

"You mean, 'made a perfect emergency landing'?" Delilah said dryly. "Yes." The plane was gone now. It had disappeared while she was still in the hospital. She hadn't asked, and Luke hadn't told her, just how he'd removed it from the pasture.

Glenna rubbed her arms and shuddered. "When I think what would have happened . . . if he hadn't been able to . . ." She turned, the anguish of contemplated tragedy etched on her face. "I don't know what I'd do if anything happened to Luke."

"I guess you must be very close," Delilah said softly.

"Close!" Glenna threw her a surprised look. "Didn't he tell you? Luke *raised* me."

"No. He didn't tell me."

"Oh, Lord, yes. Luke isn't just my brother—he's the only mother I can remember." Glenna was looking around for a place to sit. Delilah tugged a sheepskin from the pile supporting her leg and tossed it to her.

"Here, have a sheepskin," she said in the offhand manner of an old friend.

Glenna threw her a quick smile that was very like her brother's, and settled herself, tucking her long, slender legs under her and modestly arranging her skirt.

"Our mother died when I was just a baby—about a year old. Luke would have been . . . let's see, twelve, I guess." She made a face. "Do you know any twelve-year-old boys?" Delilah shook her head. "Well, let me tell you, most of them are just awful. But here was Luke, with a father who was gone most of the time and this little baby sister to take care of. When I was really little we had housekeepers, but Luke was the one who truly took care of me. I mean, he dressed me, fixed my hair, fed me, read to me—"

"Nursery rhymes!" Delilah said suddenly.

Glenna looked startled. "Well, yeah. Of course."

"Of course," Delilah murmured, closing her eyes. There was a lump in her throat and a shaky feeling in her chest.

"What is it?" Glenna asked in alarm. "Are you in pain?"

"No. I was just remembering . . . things." Things like Luke feeding her French toast and saying, "Tweet, tweet, here comes the mama bird. . . ." Luke hanging her underthings on the line and being so bewildered by her anger. "*I have a sister. . . .*" No wonder he knew all the nursery rhymes. No wonder he could cook. No wonder he looked so comfortable wearing a dish-towel apron. No wonder . . . so very many things.

She was suddenly hungry to know more about the complicated, surprising man she'd fallen in love with. She was just beginning to realize how much there was to learn about the man she'd once thought shallow, superficial. . . . Shifting eagerly on the sheepskins, she prompted breathlessly, "How about when you got older? Luke must have gone away to school. . . ."

Glenna shook her head. "He had a scholarship offer from USC, but he turned it down. It would have meant leaving me. Instead he went to the University of Houston so he could live at home. We were living in Galveston then. Our dad was working on the offshore rigs. After he died—he was killed when a platform capsized during a hurricane—we moved to the Bay Area. That's when Luke got in his graduate work at Stanford. By that time I was in high school and Luke was being both mother *and* father." She laughed suddenly, and, doubling her hands into fists, raised them above her head in a gesture of intense frustration. "He drove me crazy! He was worse than *ten* mothers and fathers! He has this . . . huge sense of responsibility, I guess, and I was very rebellious, trying to be independent. . . . Well, you can imagine."

"Yes," Delilah said with a crooked smile. "What happened? You don't seem to have any differences now."

"Oh, sure, we do!" Glenna made a face, then tilted her head thoughtfully. "What happened? Well, I guess, for one thing, I grew up. And then, I realized that it was just . . . his way of telling me he loved me. He never *says* it. But I felt it, you know? And that's what's important, don't you think?" For a moment Glenna's animated face was radiant, and touchingly young. Then she made another wry face, and laughed. "And then, I learned to tell him to knock it off when I got tired of feeling smothered. That helped a lot!"

"You mean it *works*?" Delilah asked, laughing doubtfully.

"Sometimes—though how I ever learned to do anything for myself I don't know. It's a miracle."

"What's a miracle?" Luke wanted to know, ducking under the trees, pausing to touch his sister's hair in an offhand way.

"Nothing," she told him serenely, exchanging looks with Delilah.

Delilah's heart had dropped into her stomach. When Luke moved to her side, casually touched her cheek with the backs of his fingers, and asked, "Ready to go in? It's about lunchtime," she found that she couldn't answer him. Her heart was too full for words. Full of new ideas and discoveries. Full of wonder. Full of love.

She was thinking that people have different ways of saying, "I love you." Her father had been saying it for years, but she'd heard him for the first time just a few days ago, in a hospital room.

Was that what Luke had been trying to tell her by doing things for her? Taking care of her? She hadn't heard him . . . hadn't understood . . .

When he lifted her into his arms she put her own arms around his neck and looked into his eyes. Yes, it was there, she realized. He'd been saying it for weeks, and now at last she was hearing him, loud and clear. She couldn't tell him yet, but she hoped he might see in her eyes the understanding and the forgiveness, the vow and the promise . . .

Glenna had gone. She was driving on to Tahoe to meet

her husband, John, who was in Reno at a convention. They were hoping to get in some end-of-the-season skiing.

For the first time since the accident, Luke was alone with Delilah.

He sat at the table, brooding, watching her over his coffee cup. He was remembering the morning he'd come home after his night in jail . . . the way he'd felt then . . .

A hell of a lot had happened since that morning. It would have been hard to tell her how he felt about her then. Now it seemed impossible.

Delilah was fingering the rug that covered the back of the sofa in a thoughtful sort of way. "Glenna says these are worth a lot of money," she said suddenly. "She says people would pay to learn Navaho weaving, too. I think I'll look into it. The sheep leave me a lot of time during certain months. You know, it could be the answer to my financial worries."

"Yes," Luke murmured, feeling unexpectedly depressed. "Sounds like a good idea."

"I have a good crop of lambs," she went on, "but you never know what the market's going to do. You know what I mean?"

"Yeah."

"I have you to thank, you know," she said softly.

"Me? What for?" That sure didn't sound like Delilah, he thought.

"Well, I couldn't possibly have done it without you, you must know that."

"Bull. You'd have made it one way or another. You're strong." He got up abruptly, wondering why he suddenly felt like a dog with a sore paw. "You're a fighter, 'Lilah. A winner." He paced to the window and stood looking out across the hillside toward the pasture. "I think I probably made more trouble for you than I helped." She knew very well she didn't need him, he thought. She was telling him so right now.

But I need you, he thought in a flash of self-awareness. *I need you so much*. And he no longer had any excuse to stay.

He took a deep breath and said, "My hearing's next week."

"Oh?" Her voice was soft and breathy. "And what happens then?"

He shrugged and turned to face her. "Either we get a permit to continue exploration or we don't."

"I see. And if you don't?"

"The crew . . . moves on to another area of high seismic activity. There are promising sites all through the Sierras, the Rockies, the Cascades. Even Alaska."

"Alaska?" Odd, she thought. She seemed out of breath. "And . . . will you have to go with your crew?"

"I don't *have* to stay with the crew," he said quietly. "But I probably will." He tried a smile. "Lambing's over. You don't need me here anymore. You have all the help you need from the kids, and you're getting around pretty well by yourself." He spread his hands ruefully. "I guess I'm fresh out of plausible excuses."

The silence stretched. "I can think of one," Delilah said.

The silence became thick and palpable. Luke couldn't think of anything to say. The tension in him hummed and crackled like a high-tension power line.

Finally, with a funny catch in her voice, she said, "What . . . about my bathtub?"

"Bathtub?" he echoed, feeling obtuse.

"You told me," she said patiently, "that you could hardly wait to see me in it . . . in bubbles up to my . . . chin."

He swallowed a peculiar dryness in his throat. "I did say that, didn't I?"

"Uh-huh. And I don't see how I can manage to get into that tub until I get this contraption off my leg, do you?"

"No," he murmured. "S'pose not."

"Well, then. There you are. You'll have to stay at least until my cast comes off." Unexpectedly, she yawned. Then she stretched, like an indolent cat. Luke watched the way her throat moved, and the way her breasts pushed against her T-shirt. For the first time in days he let himself wonder what she was wearing under her shirt this time.

"Hmm," she murmured, touching her lips with her fingertips. "Luke, could you help me? I think I'd like to go to bed now."

His first reaction, unbelievably, was, Bed? It was the middle of the afternoon! But he wasn't really *that* obtuse. He walked slowly toward her, wondering how it was that he could feel both vulnerable and invincible at the same time.

Her eyes never left his face. When he finally stood beside her she reached out her hand and shyly, hesitantly, touched his thigh. He felt as if she'd branded him. And for the first time in a long time, he felt *sure*.

He smiled down at her, teasing, and murmured, "It's the middle of the afternoon. . . ."

She shrugged, smiling back. "Well, at least it's not morning."

"Someday," he said with a growl, scooping her up into his arms, "I'm going to have to cure you of that particular prejudice."

"Soon, I hope," she growled back as he kissed her.

He placed her on her bed with infinite gentleness. She kept her arms around his neck, and after a long look of confirmation, he carefully stretched himself alongside her.

She laughed huskily, touching his face with her hands. "I won't break, you know."

"Be patient. This is a new experience for me." His hand moved slowly down over her throat, her breasts, lifted the bottom edge of her T-shirt, and lay warmly on her soft stomach.

"What is? Making love to someone with a broken leg?" Her voice was breaking up into shivering little fragments of speech.

"That too. No, I meant . . . being seduced . . ."

"Seduced!" She slapped at his hand in mild outrage. "I did not! What a thing to say. I'd never—"

" 'Lilah," he said. "Don't argue."

Her voice deserted her when he put his mouth where his hand had been.

"Isn't it strange, the way things happen? . . ." Delilah's voice was a fuzzy purr in his ear. He was lying on his stomach, with his head pillowed on her stomach, listening to her body sounds . . . an unbelievably pleasant and reassuring intimacy.

"Like what, love?" he murmured, moving his head to touch a kiss below her ribs.

Her fingers stirred in his hair. "I don't know. Fate, I guess."

"Thought you didn't believe in fate."

"I didn't used to. But . . ." Her voice caught and took on the subtle tensions of fear. "Oh, Luke. Do you know how close I came to throwing this away? That morning—remember?—when you hung my things on the line, and I was going to take you to town, but the pickup wouldn't start? Just think, if it hadn't been for that stupid pickup, you wouldn't have stayed. And it never had done that before, and it's never done it since. If that isn't some kind of fate, what is it?"

Luke was silent, and very still. After a moment she prodded him, rocking his head impatiently back and forth. "Luke? Isn't that something to make you think?"

"No." He pressed his face into the golden velvet of her stomach and sighed, then resolutely pushed himself away and propped himself on one elbow. "It makes me . . . I have a confession to make."

Delilah raised herself on her elbows, and said with a dark foreboding, "Oh, no."

"Yes. I'm afraid fate had nothing to do with the pickup not starting. I . . . um, sort of made an adjustment in the engine."

"A *what*? Luke, what did you do?"

"I took out the rotor. You know, from the distributor . . ."

She gave a fierce, incredulous stare, while his heart

hung in delicate balance. Suddenly she flopped back onto the pillows and began to shake with laughter.

He watched her quizzically, still not certain enough of her, or familiar enough with her moods, to risk joining in.

"Oh, Luke." She sighed, wiping her face with both hands. "You really are devious."

"No," he said. "Just determined. Forgive me?"

Her hand touched his arm, then slid across his rib cage to rest like a tender blessing right over his heart. "Of course," she said simply. "I love you. And besides . . ." Her fingers curled abruptly and withdrew. "I . . . sort of have a confession to make too."

"Oh?" He made a valiant effort to sound stern. "What's that?"

She propped her head on one arm and regarded him somberly. "I'm not *really* allergic to cigarette smoke. I—I just don't like it." Her voice rose with alarm as he slowly sat up. "And I was just . . . being contrary, I guess. But if you really, really have to smoke, I don't mind. I mean . . . well, I do mind, because it's so bad for you, and it gives you wrinkles and yellow teeth, and I know I *said* you were too beautiful, but Mara Jane was right, I have gotten used to it, and it seems such a shame—*Luke!*"

His name was a breathless squawk as he caught her to him and held her hard against his chest. He felt the softness and warmth of her breasts meld with the hair-roughened contours of his body. He barely had breath enough to growl, "You talk too much!" before he kissed her.

After a while he sighed and tucked her head into the hollow of his neck. "Oh, 'Lilah . . ." he whispered, taking a breath. "How I love you."

It was amazing how easy it was to say it at last—as natural and right as drawing a breath.

THE EDITOR'S CORNER

If there were a theme for next month's LOVESWEPT romances, it might be "Pennies from Heaven," because in all four books something wonderful seems to drop from above right into the lives of our heroes or heroines.

First, in Peggy Webb's utterly charming **DONOVAN'S ANGEL,** LOVESWEPT #143, Martie Fleming tumbles down (literally) into Paul Donovan's garden. Immediately fascinated by Martie, Paul feels she is indeed a blessing straight from heaven—an especially appropriate notion as he's a minister. But, discovering his vocation, Martie runs for cover, convinced that she is so unconventional she could never be a clergyman's wife. Most of the parishioners seem to agree: her spicy wit and way-out clothes and unusual occupation set their tongues wagging. Paul, determined as he is to have Martie, seems fated to lose . . . until a small miracle or two intervenes. You simply can't let yourself miss this funny, heartwarming love story that so perfectly captures the atmosphere of a small Southern town.

The very title of our next romance, **WILD BLUE YONDER,** LOVESWEPT #144, by Millie Grey, gives you a clue to how it fits our theme. Mike Donahue pilots an antique biplane like a barnstormer of years gone by. And when he develops engine trouble and lands on Krissa Colbrook's property, he's soon devel-

(continued)

oping trouble for her too . . . trouble of the heart. The last kind of man placid Krissa needs or wants in her life is a daredevil, yet she falls hard for this irresistible vagabond who's come to her from the sky above. We think it would be hard for a reader to fail to be charmed by Mike, so we feel secure in saying that you will be enchanted by the way Mike goes about ridding Krissa of her fears!

For just a second now try to put yourself into the very large shoes of one Morgan Abbott, hero of talented newcomer Linda Cajio's **ALL IS FAIR . . .**, LOVESWEPT #145. Imagine that you (you're that handsome Morgan, remember?) are having dinner with acquaintances when an absolutely stunning beauty—who is also a perfect stranger—rushes up and kisses you passionately before quickly disappearing. Then, another day in another city, the same gorgeous lady again appears suddenly, kisses you senseless and vanishes. Wouldn't your head be reeling? Well, those are just two of the several unique ways that Cecilia St. Martin gets to Abbott. You will relish this wildly wonderful, very touching romance from Linda who makes her truly stylish, truly nifty debut as a romance writer with us.

And last, but never, never least is the beautiful romance **JOURNEY'S END,** LOVESWEPT #146, by Joan Elliott Pickart. In this dramatic and tender love story Victoria Blair finds everything she ever dreamed of having in the arms of Sage Lawson, owner of the Lazy L ranch just outside Sunshine, New Mexico. Indeed at times sunshine does seem to pour down on these two lovely people who appear to be made in heaven for each other. Yet ominous clouds of doubt and misunderstanding threaten their budding love. Sage

(continued)

grows hostile, Blair becomes distant, withdrawn. Clearly they need a little push back into one another's arms . . . and the matchmakers and the ways they give that little push are sure to delight you.

As always, we hope that each of these four LOVE-SWEPTs will give you the greatest of pleasure.

With warm good wishes,

Carolyn Nichols

Carolyn Nichols
Editor
LOVESWEPT
Bantam Books, Inc.
666 Fifth Avenue
New York, NY 10103

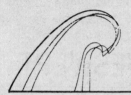 **LOVESWEPT**

Love Stories you'll never forget by authors you'll always remember

 # LOVESWEPT

*Love Stories you'll never forget
by authors you'll always remember*

☐	21708	**Out of This World #103** Nancy Holder	$2.25
☐	21699	**Rachel's Confession #107** Fayrene Preston	$2.25
☐	21716	**A Tough Act to Follow #108** Billie Green	$2.25
☐	21718	**Come As You Are #109** Laurien Berenson	$2.25
☐	21719	**Sunlight's Promise #110** Joan Elliott Pickart	$2.25
☐	21726	**Dear Mitt #111** Sara Orwig	$2.25
☐	21729	**Birds Of A Feather #112** Peggy Web	$2.25
☐	21727	**A Matter of Magic #113** Linda Hampton	$2.25
☐	21728	**Rainbow's Angel #114** Joan Elliott Pickart	$2.25

Prices and availability subject to change without notice.

Buy them at your local bookstore or use this handy coupon for ordering: